REMEMBER WHEN

PREETHI VENUGOPALA

Copyright © Preethi Venugopala
All Rights Reserved.

Contents

1. Chapter 1 — 1
2. Chapter 2 — 9
3. Chapter 3 — 15
4. Chapter 4 — 20
5. Chapter 5 — 27
6. Chapter 6 — 32
7. Chapter 7 — 41
8. Chapter 8 — 46
9. Chapter 9 — 51
10. Chapter 10 — 59
11. Chapter 11 — 66
12. Chapter 12 — 72
13. Chapter 13 — 77
14. Chapter 14 — 84
15. Chapter 15 — 92
16. Chapter 16 — 98
17. Chapter 17 — 104
18. Chapter 18 — 114
19. Chapter 19 — 120
20. Chapter 20 — 126
21. Chapter 21 — 131
22. Chapter 22 — 136
23. Chapter 23 — 141
24. Chapter 24 — 146

Contents

25. Chapter 25   152

26. Chapter 26   158

27. Chapter 27   165

28. Chapter 28   171

29. Chapter 29   180

30. Chapter 30   188

Author's Note   193

Acknowledgements   195

Blurbs Of Novels By Preethi Venugopala   197

Other Works By The Author   217

1

———◆♡◆———

September 23, 2015, Bangalore

"Remember when I was young and so were you..."

Tara swayed listening to the sound of Alan Jackson's soothing voice as she chopped veggies. *Remembering...* wasn't that what she did best? Living in the moment, *carpe diem* never worked for her. She didn't live in the present or seize the day as they said.

She remembered.

She wallowed in the past.

She couldn't help it. The past had left deep scars on her.

Also, God had bestowed her with an elephantine memory. She remembered everything. Crystal clear. There were neatly labelled, organized compartments in her brain that made it easy for her to recall anything on command. Especially the painful memories. One day her over-worked brain cells might decide that enough was enough and just conk off.

Were her genes the culprits? Her mother picked fights with her father quoting his mistakes from as far back as the 1970s.

A shrill ringtone sounded, cutting off the singer's soothing baritone. 'SisterR calling' flashed on the mobile screen and Tara tensed.

What did Ranjini, the human version of a migraine, want now? The extra R in sisterR on Tara's phone didn't represent the first letter of her sister's name. Tara had added it to remind herself that picking her call was going to be a mistake, an error.

Tara let it ring, not wanting to answer it. Yet, knowing what might follow if she didn't answer, Tara swiped the answer icon. A phone call was safer than a live confrontation.

"Why the heck did you answer so late?" Ranjini's voice blared from the cell phone's speaker.

Tara had all the mind to shower the expletives that arrived on the tip of her tongue on her obnoxious sister. But biting back the retorts, Tara said, "I was busy in the kitchen."

"Why don't you keep a cook? It is not like you can't afford one. Do you want me to send one?"

"You know I love to cook. And we are just three people. We don't need much."

"Even then, you should appoint people to do such menial works. I am sure Karthik would agree. The world around can be easily managed nowadays with the click of a button." She proceeded to explain how she accomplished it all armed with just her smartphone. Maids, beauticians, concert tickets, designer dresses, flashy heels... the world became her marketplace with just a click on the 'Add to Cart' button.

Tara's lips curled into a smile. When would Ranjini realize that unlike her, Tara didn't have parties to attend, didn't shop until she dropped or went globe-trotting every month? She half-listened as she transferred the veggies into the skillet, added sauces, and tossed.

"Why did you call?" Tara asked, interrupting her sister's long lifestyle speech.

"Can't I call my sister?" Ranjini's voice sounded coarse. After another tirade, which lasted a few minutes, she quickly switched back into her bragging mode. She began to describe in detail her latest vacation to St Tropez, a beautiful getaway in the South of France. Shopping, admirers, moonlit beaches, exotic meals and other interesting vignettes tumbled out of her mouth one after the other.

"You should go there. It's amazing," Ranjini concluded.

Karthik and Tara never went on vacations. Their only trips were to Kannur, their hometown, to visit their families. Even those were brief. Karthik was busy all the time. She knew Ranjini was trying to rile her as Tara loved to travel.

"Tell me, how is your work progressing?" Ranjini asked when Tara continued to remain silent.

"It is going well. I am currently editing the manuscript as per the feedback from the editor—."

"Darling, darling... I am afraid I've to cut short our conversation. I am getting a call on the other line. Unlike you, I am a very busy woman, remember? See you."

Tara wished she could pour a bucket of ice water on Ranjini. Couldn't she at least change her parting dialogue? Ranjini called her only when she wanted to boast about her oh-so colourful life and make Tara feel awful. Such a waste of time and energy!

Though Tara's life wasn't dreary, she had Ranjini to thank for whatever little regret that lay buried in her heart. Ranjini found a way to prod it out whenever she called.

Tara disconnected the call fighting the urge to smash the phone against the countertop.

Movies or stories where siblings bonded with one another often made her wonder if such things occurred in real life. She had only experienced sibling rivalry.

The more she tried to bond with Ranjini, the farther she drifted away. Initially, Tara had dismissed it as her imagination. It had taken her a long time to understand that she would never have Ranjini as a friend. It was as if she perceived Tara as a threat - a threat to her very existence.

Tara switched off the flame after checking the salt and spice. She sank onto the couch in the living room and distracted herself via social media.

An article about the depleting Amazon rainforest cover grabbed her attention. The images of lakes, mountains and trees transported her back to her college days. Particularly to their nature club trips where they wandered around in dense forests collecting rare plant specimens, battled against leeches while playing hide and seek with predators.

Along with it came another set of memories. Laughter, bonfires, music and ...love. Her world had been rosy then.

The clock on the wall chimed reminding her it was time to go and pick up Aryan from school. Battling the Bangalore traffic took a toll on her and she reached five minutes late.

Aryan, her five-year-old, was waiting in the school lobby along with a few other students. Tara smiled at him and he beamed at her. He waved goodbye to his friends and ran to her. Tara kept his bag in the back seat of the car and waited until he climbed in.

Leaning back against the seat, he confessed, "I fought with Aditi today."

"Why?" Tara asked, knowing further revelations would follow.

"She said you would beat me today. You would never do that, would you?"

"Should I?" Tara asked.

"Mothers should never beat their babies. Aayush rubbed his dirty palms on my trousers. It wasn't my mistake," he protested. His lips trembled and tears began to accumulate in his eyes.

Tara let out an exasperated sigh as she inspected his trousers. Dirt had turned the otherwise white shorts into a dirty orange. Yet the tears blinking in Aryan's eyes made her smile.

"Don't cry, my baby. I won't beat you. Mommy loves you, right?" Tara said, wiping his tears, which had by now tumbled out of his eyes.

"And I love you," he said and sobbed. They were sobs of relief. Tara kissed his cheeks and hugged him.

"Mommy, will you hug me always?" he asked.

"I will."

"Aayush says big boys don't hug their mothers. He doesn't, it seems."

"You can always hug me. Even after I turn into a grey old woman." Tara sighed thinking how vulnerable kids were. Anyone could plant seeds of doubt in their tender mind.

"I don't want you to turn into an old woman. You are my mother." Aryan bawled.

"Okay. Okay. I won't. Now, shall we go?" He nodded. Tara wished it were true. She was twenty-eight. A few silver lines had already started appearing among her hair. But if she showed them to her five-year-old, it would be enough to start another sobbing session.

As she was about to slip into the driving seat, someone tapped on her shoulder.

"Tara! What a pleasant surprise."

Tara turned around and squealed in delight. "Oh my God, Rupa. I can't believe it is you. Long time. You haven't changed much."

"But you have become more beautiful. What hair, what curves, my dear!" Rupa said. To Tara's horror, Rupa patted her buttocks.

Tara rolled her eyes and laughed. The last time they had been in each other's company, Tara was the one who had short hair. Now Rupa sported a stylish bob whereas Tara's hair touched her hips.

"You never change, do you? We are on the road, idiot. Tell me, what brings you to Bangalore? When did you return from Boston?" Tara asked.

"I'm here to attend an entrepreneur's conference at this hotel," she quipped, indicating the star hotel adjacent to Aryan's school. "I'm an entrepreneur now, can you believe that?"

"Of course, I can believe it. It's such great news. What business do you do?"

"I have set up an international business selling Kerala art murals. They are a rage abroad." Rupa handed over a business card for 'Malabar Art Murals' to Tara. Her website address, phone number and other contact details were beautifully inscribed on it.

Tara used to be a frequent visitor to her house while in college. Rupa's family had many artists. The murals in many of their local temples were their creations. And now she was taking their art to the world. "Good job. I am proud of you."

"Who is this, Mommy?" Aryan asked, peeking out through the car window.

"This is mommy's best friend from college, Aryan. Rupa, meet my son, my hero, Aryan," Tara said and Aryan grinned at Rupa pleased by the introduction.

"Hello, Aryan. You are so cute," said Rupa.

Oh, oh, the wrong thing to say. Tara shook her head and mouthed a 'no' to Rupa.

"I am not cute. I am smart. Girls are cute," Aryan declared with a scowl.

"How silly of me! You are not cute at all. You are smart," Rupa corrected, determined to maintain peace. Peace was reestablished. She rummaged through her bag and took out a Cadburys Dairy Milk bar.

"This is my hello gift to you," she said. Aryan looked at Tara for consent and with her permission accepted the chocolate.

"I guess your event is over. Hop in. Come home," Tara said, glancing at the hotel from where people were streaming out in batches.

"No time, dear. Actually, I am in a bit of a hurry," she said.

"Okay. When can we meet then?"

"Can't say yet. Give me your number. I'll message you. And by the way, how is Manu?" she asked.

"I don't know," Tara said, caught unaware by the question. Rupa's eyes widened and flitted between Aryan and Tara.

"Come home, Rupa. Karthik would love to meet you," Tara said.

"You married Karthik? Your Karthik?" she asked.

Tara nodded and Rupa's fingers flew to her lips.

"But why?" she asked.

"It's complicated," Tara said and Rupa grabbed her hands.

"I can't breathe till I hear all about it. I am coming with you. Give me a minute," she said. She called someone and then got into Tara's car without a word.

While Tara drove home, they talked in codes trying to keep their secrets from Aryan. Once Aryan slept after tea and snacks, Tara bared her heart to Rupa.

"This is so bizarre. I knew your sister was a bitch. But to this extent.... I'm so sorry, Tara. I didn't know. And Manu?"

"It's okay. Perhaps it was not meant to be. I'm happy now. I have Aryan. And Karthik is a good person. He understands me. He cares for me," Tara said.

"Care? Understand? Is that enough?"

"It is," Tara said.

Tara could see other questions Rupa wished to ask hiding behind the many aborted attempts to return to the story she knew. For a moment, Tara wished she hadn't met her.

Manu's name had never been uttered in this house before. Yet it had always floated around, like a forbidden word, hiding behind thoughts, embroiled in a mesh of what-ifs. When the truth was bitter and nothing changed it, no matter how hard one tried, it was better to leave it alone.

When Tara closed the door behind Rupa, who left after promising to call soon, Tara wished she had not talked about it at all. It was not going to serve any purpose.

2

It was ten in the evening. Aryan was busy with his iPad. Screams of angry birds filled the living room.

"Mommy, finish this level," Aryan said handing the tablet to Tara. She imagined the pigs to be her sister and threw birds at them tactfully. She won the level easily and passed the iPad to Aryan who praised her for being such a brilliant player. Then he darted out of the room leaving Tara alone with her thoughts.

A minute later, he came into the room howling in distress, followed by Karthik who had lathered his face with shaving foam.

"Mummy, please help me," he begged and hid behind her. The duo would drive her mad. This scene was repeated every night and yet, they never tired of it. The big man kept teasing the little one who never thought of it as a prank.

"Don't guard him. This time I am determined to make a man out of him. Give him up. He will have his moustache shaved," Karthik said.

Usually, Tara would have played along and pleaded not to harass her little one. Karthik would then act as if he was giving in to her pleas and Aryan would hail her as his benevolent protector and call her the best mother in the world. Today, the whole act irritated Tara.

"Karthik, grow up," Tara snapped. Pushing Karthik out of her path, she exited the room. Aryan followed, giggling but impressed by this heroic, new avatar of his usually submissive mommy.

Karthik appeared in their bedroom half an hour later, his face scrubbed and clean. Tara always found his habit of shaving every night before going to bed weird.

"If all my clothes were wrinkle-free, I would have worn them to bed too. Then I could just walk to the office after brushing my teeth. I hate shaving, ironing, and getting ready in the morning. Corporate life sucks," he had explained after they had moved to Bangalore three years ago.

According to him, his job as the senior legal manager in an MNC demanded that he look good. His office clothes were laundry pressed and everything about his appearance screamed class. Like everything else, their style sense did not match. Tara preferred comfort, rather than style or trend.

An hour later, Tara was sitting cross-legged on her bed, reading her manuscript from her laptop. Aryan lay next to her watching a nursery rhyme on YouTube. She looked up and when Karthik smiled, unintentionally a scowl appeared on her face.

"Why are you so grumpy today? Anything wrong? Aryan mentioned your friend came home today. Who was it?"

"Rupa."

"Mmm. That explains everything. Are we back to square one then?"

Tara kept mum. Tossing his bath towel into the laundry basket, Karthik turned to walk out of the room when Aryan who was ready for bed called out to him.

"Come here, Daddy. You know I can't sleep if I'm not lying between you and Mummy. I'm sleepy."

Karthik pasted a smile on his face and climbed onto the bed. Shutting down her laptop, Tara kept it on the nightstand. After switching off the other lights, she turned on the night lamp. She lay beside Aryan who immediately threw one leg on her and snuggled against her.

"You smell so good, Mummy," he said and kissed her cheek. Tara listened as he rambled about his friends, angry birds, and school. Soon, he asked her to sing a lullaby. By the time she sang the first few lines of his favourite one, he fell asleep.

Karthik who had remained silent all along immediately got up and returned to his bedroom. Tara sat up on the bed pondering about her life, past and present and the other side of the bed, which always remained empty. She had no one else but herself to blame for the mess called her life. Her impulsiveness had left in its wake broken hearts and lives, including her own.

To forget reality, she took refuge in the study room proofreading her manuscript until drowsiness began to blur the letters. Bookmarking the location, she returned to bed. Hugging Aryan she fell asleep immediately.

Hours later, she woke suffocated by sobs born out of a dream about Manu. He'd appeared haggard and heartbroken.

Where was he? Did he even remember her? Perhaps somewhere right at this moment, he was awake and thinking ill about her, hating her. Anguished tears filled her eyes.

Pushing open the bedroom window, Tara watched the moon shining brightly. There was a time when a single glance at the moon filled her with peace. Today, it made her miserable, reminding her of happier times.

Time had taken away everything she loved, leaving scars of love deep within her heart. The carefree days full of promise were long gone. Nowadays bitter regret blighted her days and sadness ruled her nights.

One mistake had ruined it all. Secrets, which longed to come out into the open, usurped her heart. They terrified her with visuals of the terrible outcomes when the truth finally came out.

Tara typed Manu's full name in the Google search box on her phone. It didn't turn up any results as usual. People believed it was easy to trace individuals in this digital age. But if one was determined to avoid the public eye, it was entirely possible. Manu was the proof. He had deleted his Facebook and Orkut accounts after the social media humiliation he had undergone five years ago. All thanks to her.

Tara wished she could return to those days when not a day passed without them posting photos and messages on each other's timelines. They chatted long into the night. Sometimes they debated on serious topics they cared about and sometimes they were just two young lovers dreaming of a future together.

Now she didn't even know whether he was alive. His family had left Kannur immediately after the scandal.

Tara tossed and turned for hours and then fell into a fretful sleep. When she woke up, her bed was empty. The clock on the nightstand showed that it was ten in the morning. Oh God, how could she sleep so late on a school day?

Yet, the house was silent. Strange sounding creatures didn't speak from the television, nor did she hear screams of angry birds. She was alone in the house. Puzzled, she searched the house for Aryan. On the dining table, a note awaited her.

Didn't think of disturbing you. You appeared exhausted. I am taking Aryan to school. I will buy him some cupcakes from the cafeteria below for his lunch box. He drank his glass of milk with Horlicks and ate some biscuits. I took care of everything, right? You take a rest. See you in the evening.

-Karthik.

The message made Tara feel guilty all over again. What kind of a mother and wife was she? She needed to stop obsessing over the past and ruining her present.

The most toxic poison in the world was guilt. It acted on the human psyche like acid and destroyed it silently from within. Within seconds, Tara felt crestfallen. Her world was crumpling around her. She felt like running away.

An email from her editor reminding her to finish the proofreading as soon as possible became the wake-up call she needed. Deadlines were real. After a long leisurely bath and a strong coffee, Tara plunged herself into proofreading.

If all went as planned, her first novel would be published on the 25th of November, 2015. A long-cherished dream.

This story had found her when she had been depressed and lonely. Creating a fictional world filled with love had healed her. She'd felt as if the characters were real. They spoke to her. She could relate to their plight. After finishing the first draft, she had started polishing the manuscript and embellishing it with details.

A popular publisher had picked it up for publishing after a random query. After being homebound for a long time, she had found her real passion in storytelling. Other than the novel, she had a few short stories published in some online literary magazines.

Tara had started blogging a long while ago. It had initially been her secret sanctum to dump her worries. Now she had upgraded her blog into her author website. She posted short stories every Saturday. It had created an ever-growing readership base.

If she could believe their comments, her readers were eagerly waiting for her book. It gave her tiny moments of anxiety when she wondered whether her book would live up to their expectations.

Tara's editor, Aparna, often sent her invitations to book events in and around Bangalore. She forced her to attend them to give her a glimpse into the life of writers. However, instead of giving her confidence, each event had killed her eagerness for her book launch.

The audience disappointed her. The only saving grace was the presence of one or two sincere bibliophiles. Mostly the crowd was filled with pseudo-intellectuals and snobs who used the opportunity to show off their knowledge. Some struggling writers turned up only to humiliate the authors. Some newbie authors turned up and used such events to plug in their books.

Considering the online popularity of her stories, her publishers were planning four major launches. One in Delhi, one in Bangalore, one in Kolkata and one in Chennai.

The first launch was to be in Chennai as her story was based there. She had selected the place as the background for her story as she had spent the greater part of her childhood there. Chennai was close to her heart, unlike any other place. Bangalore was a second home and Kannur, the land of folklores and looms in Kerala, held her roots.

3

2015, December 1, Chennai

Manu had never seen it rain so heavily. Not once since he had first come to Chennai for his PhD five years ago. The traffic was moving at a snail's pace through the flooded roads. He had to reach the Starmark bookstore in Chennai by four-thirty. It was already four and he still had a few kilometres to go.

His friend Aparna had called him this morning with an unusual request. Aparna worked as an editor at a publishing company.

"You have to moderate this book launch. The person who was supposed to do it cannot make it to the event. The book is a well-written romance and the author is pretty."

"Is this another attempt to get me a date? I am fed up with your matchmaking tactics."

"Take a chill pill, Manu. This girl is happily married with a child. I wouldn't have bothered you if our moderator could attend. You are my last resort. Please, put up your best face and be there half an hour before the launch. I will brief you."

Manu worked as a senior science editor for sciencereporter.com, an online science portal. Because of his job, he was often invited to book events. He was a regular in the book circles. He loved reading and it was not restricted to non-fiction books. A good thriller or a fantasy was his go-to genre to relax after a hectic day. Anything that could stop his mind from wandering into unwanted territories was welcome.

Aparna greeted him at the office of the bookstore and guided him to a chair.

"Please don't intimidate the author just because you don't like the genre. Be considerate. She is a newbie," said Aparna.

"Do I ever do that? I try to be friendly. Always."

"This is the book summary," said Aparna handing over a sheet of paper.

Manu speed read the book summary. It seemed fine. A love story about second chances in love. He didn't believe in love or second chances. Love was one huge deception.

"This is the book you will be launching. Just read through the author bio. It will give you enough material to prepare your introduction."

The book's cover and title were impressive. 'Summer Dreams'. The cover featured a few Mayflower blossoms scattered on a lawn. The blue sky beyond highlighted the title. When he read the name of the author, he stiffened. Tara Vasudevan.

With slight trepidation, he opened the book and searched for the author pic. A familiar face stared straight at him from the back page. Tara, his Tara. No, not his Tara anymore. The bio mentioned she lived in Bangalore with her husband and son.

She had changed. Her hair was longer, and overall, she seemed better groomed and happier. Anger and hatred bubbled inside him. All the hurt that he had struggled to forget over the years threatened to surface. He wished he could throw the book in a bin and walk away.

Wiping the unexpected beads of perspiration from his forehead, he looked around. Aparna was busy giving last-minute instructions to the store manager. Did she know?

But, how could she? He had never told anyone about Tara. He had left his past where it belonged: firmly in the past.

It was another story that he still dreamed about her. Dreams that left him drained and struggling to breathe. Should he tell Aparna he couldn't do it? After all his attempts to forget her, fate had suddenly thrown her in his path again.

Perhaps, he should tell Aparna. Just then, a tiny voice sounded in the room.

"Is this the place where your book will be launched, Mummy?"

"Yes, sweetheart. But you should not talk so loudly here. It is like a library, okay?"

Manu sat firmly in the chair and avoided looking in the direction of the voices. He had not forgotten anything about her. Memories came in like a hurricane. He shut his eyes firmly and took a calming breath. It was time to face her. He, at least, had got a warning. He would love to surprise her. So, he stood up and turned to face her.

"Hello, Tara. Wonderful to meet you after all these years," he said. He moved closer, smiled at her and offered his hand for a formal handshake.

Her face blanched. Her hands had gone cold. He was enjoying this confrontation immensely. He didn't think it was true for her. She looked as if she would faint.

"Hey there, buddy. What is your name?" he addressed her son.

The kid beamed up at him and said, 'Aryan.'

Somewhere within him, something churned and then formed a knot of regret. This could have been his child. That thought sent another wave of anger coursing through him and he bit his inner cheek.

"Oh, so you both know each other? That makes it all so much better," Aparna said.

She had no idea how difficult that made everything. He smiled at her.

"I guess you will want to refresh yourself before the launch, Tara. There is a restroom right there. We will meet you in ten minutes, Manu."

Aparna led Tara out of the room. Manu sat down and leafed through her book, repeatedly, not reading even a single word. Her face played in front of his eyes and he struggled to keep calm. He couldn't wait to be back in the comfort of his house and forget all about this. Ugh! Why had he agreed to this launch?

Minutes later, Tara reentered the room. She looked composed. Her saree hugged her enticing curves and her skin glowed. Her hair now almost reached her hips. She had become even more beautiful. What was the emotion clawing at his heart? Regret? Despair?

"Buy me that angry birds plush toy that is displayed at the window, okay? Then I promise, I will be a good boy," Aryan declared. Aparna laughed. Tara rolled her eyes.

"I will buy it for you if you prove that you are a good boy, okay?"

"Pinky promise?"

"Pinky promise," Tara said and linked her pinky finger with his.

With a smile, Tara looked up and met Manu's eyes but immediately looked away. Aryan continued chatting and asking clever but innocent questions. He demanded a storybook so that he could be a good kid throughout the launch. Aparna walked towards the window display and picked a Disney Princess story collection. Aryan refused to accept it.

"I want that book about the Octonauts. I love Octonauts. They teach me stuff about the ocean."

Manu was finding the kid adorable with every passing minute. Aparna handed him the book.

"I am sorry. Karthik couldn't make it to the launch. Some last-minute meeting came up and he had to go. If he were here, he would have taken care of Aryan," said Tara.

Oh, so she had married her cousin Karthik, the one she used to talk about frequently, the nerd in their family. Manu ground his teeth. He couldn't stand hearing her gloat about her happily married life.

"I think I might need an ice cream as well if I need to keep quiet. I don't talk when I eat, do I, Mommy?"

Manu chuckled hearing the new demand and walked out of the room. He returned after a while holding a big red angry-bird plush and a cup of chocolate ice cream.

"Wow! Thank you. How did you know I liked chocolate and angry birds?" Aryan asked eagerly, accepting his gifts.

"I know what smart boys like," Manu said and winked at him.

4

Tara had been looking forward to the book launch for months. Yet now, when it was happening, she was in a stupor of sorts. All thanks to the man who was sitting next to her.

She was on autopilot and not fully aware of anything happening around her. She did what she was supposed to do. She answered the random questions that were thrown at her both by the audience and by Manu. She also read out from her book and signed copies for those who had bought her book.

Manu had not changed much in appearance. But his attitude towards her had undergone a sea change. The lover who cherished her presence had transformed into a stranger who made her feel unwanted.

Manu's questions during the launch had felt personal to her.

"Why do you write romance?"

"Do you believe in true love?"

Tara didn't remember her answers. She had faced the audience when she answered them. Whenever their eyes had met, Manu's eyes asked her a thousand questions for which she had no answers. Together with guilt, regret held her heart in an icy grip.

All through the function, she prayed for a chance to ask him for forgiveness. He soon left her on the stage to allow the readers to get the books signed. Tara watched him stealthily whenever she got the chance. If he had slipped away, she might have abandoned all pretence and ran after him.

Much to her relief, he didn't leave. Maybe he wanted to talk too. He kept standing, hands in his pocket staring around as if bored by whatever was happening. The next time when she looked up, he was gesturing to Aryan to go to him. Aryan pulled at her saree, asking for permission. When she nodded a yes, he ran toward Manu, clutching his angry bird plush toy.

When Tara glanced up next, Manu who was listening to Aryan's babble, burst out laughing. The sound sent a shudder of excitement through her. She had not forgotten his laugh. The deep, hearty sound always did strange things to her heart. It had been one of the first things that had endeared him to her.

After signing the copy for the last person in the queue, Tara stood up. It was time to face him. Their plane was scheduled to leave at 8:40. Because of the rain, the travel time from the airport to Starmark had taken an hour. Allowing that much time, she still had a little over an hour to spend with him.

An hour to compensate for all the yearning and longing over the years. An hour to right all the wrongs she had done.

Years ago, hours flew away like seconds whenever they were together. They had taken time for granted. Youth made one reckless. Unfortunately, she didn't have the luxury of time now. The ticking clock announced that the hours were racing past. All she would have if she wasted this one hour would be a pile of rusty regrets.

With a wan smile pasted on her face, Tara approached Manu who was deep in conversation with Aparna. His face clouded when he saw her.

"I am so glad it all went well. Thanks a ton for all the help, Manu. I guess, being college mates, you would probably want to catch up. Tara, shall I leave you in Manu's company? Manu, be a sweetheart and see to it that she reaches the airport on time. I don't know what time I will be able to get to the dinner party at my in-laws' place because of this rain," said Aparna.

"Don't worry about anything. You go," said Manu. Aparna hugged Tara and bid her goodbye and exited briskly from the hall. Manu had turned away from Tara. She wondered if the thought of being alone with her troubled him. Silence hung heavily between them. Tara struggled to find the words that could establish a semblance of peace between them.

"Mummy, I want something to eat. I am hungry," Aryan said as he handed the angry bird over to her. Tara held it in her hands and looked around.

"Do you like pizza?" Manu asked.

The answer from Aryan was a whopping 'yes' and the two walked away hand-in-hand without even bothering to ask her opinion. Tara followed them silently, wording and rewording in her mind the apology she owed to Manu. She had wronged him. She wondered how he had tolerated her presence till now. If she was in his place, she might have escaped hours ago.

The food court was on the third floor of the mall which housed the bookstore. Aryan yelped in glee when he saw the kiosk of his favourite pizza outlet. Soon they were sitting around a round table waiting for their pizza.

"Mama, can I have my tablet? I want to play angry birds while I wait." Tara rummaged through her bag and took the iPad out. Switching it on, she gave it to Aryan who immediately swiped the screen and clicked on the game icon. The angry birds' theme music streamed out from the tablet. Within minutes, Aryan became engrossed in his game.

This was her opportunity to speak. Yet, she dreaded to begin. Tears were beginning to sting at the back of her eyes. Letting out a deep breath, she leaned toward Manu.

"I am sorry, Manu. You didn't deserve any of the things that happened to you," Tara mumbled, lowering her voice.

Manu moved away quickly restoring the space between them.

"Do you think that is enough? An apology would right everything?" He snapped. His eyes were glowing like embers.

His words stung. As if he couldn't bear to be near her anymore, he stood up and wandered away to the food counter. Nothing she would say would bring whatever they had back. Whatever she was attempting to do was too little, too late. Her heart squeezed. She wiped a teardrop that had slipped out.

Her phone pinged and she opened the message that had come in. It was from her airline. A flight cancellation message. What?

Tara called the help desk of the airline to get transferred to a later flight.

"No, ma'am. We are very sorry. All flights have been cancelled due to severe flooding at the airport. The airport has been closed down temporarily. We don't know when the flights will be operational."

"But..."

"We will refund the full amount, ma'am. Sorry for the trouble. Is there anything else we can help you with?" After thanking the girl, Tara disconnected the call.

A crowd had gathered around the nearby television screen. The scenes and breaking news along with the recent call made the reality of her situation crystal clear. She was stranded in a strange place that was suddenly facing a flood situation.

Manu turned around to look at her when the television at the kiosk showed footage of the flooded airport. The breaking news banner proclaimed that Chennai airport was temporarily shut down. Her panic must have shown on her face because he immediately returned to their table. Manu enquired about the status of her flight.

"Cancelled. I don't know what to do now."

"Don't worry. We will find a way out. I will make sure that you reach Bangalore safely." There was no sign of the anger that had burned in his eyes minutes ago. She was seeing glimpses of the youth she had loved. Trustworthy and dependable in any situation.

By the time their pizza arrived, Tara had lost her appetite. She sat watching Aryan and Manu eat, brooding about how a day that had begun on a bad note was going steadily downhill.

Karthik had promised to accompany them for the book launch. He had cancelled at the last moment as some urgent work had come up in the office. Unlike her usual self, she had lost it and raged at him. All her suppressed angst had come out. She had held him responsible even for the unhappy state of their marriage. She had momentarily forgotten how he had been her saviour when things had turned murky. Yet, it seemed to have set the mood of the day. Meeting Manu, facing his ire and now this flood situation.

Tara tried calling Karthik. It was still repeating the same message. His phone was switched off. Perhaps he was giving her the space to think. He had called her to apologise when they were waiting to board the flight. And then he had made a startling demand. Could she ever accede to that?

Now was not the time to find an answer to any such questions. She needed to find a way to return to Bangalore.

Upon enquiry, they found that either the buses were all full or they were cancelled. Several routes were inaccessible as many bridges were underwater.

Maybe she should find a place to stay. Once the flights started operating, she could travel. She would have to buy some necessary supplies as she was not prepared for an overnight stay.

"Is there a garment store nearby? I will have to stay at a nearby hotel till the flights resume."

"Okay. There are many stores in this mall. After that, we will find a good hotel for you," Manu said.

At the clothes showroom there, Tara purchased two pairs of night suits and two kurtas, leggings and essential innerwear. For Aryan, she purchased five pairs of T-shirts and trousers as he was in the habit of muddying his clothes often. Given the severity of the floods, it might take days for the flights to be operational.

Next, they hunted for a place to stay. Every hotel Manu took them to was full owing to the many flights, trains and buses that had got cancelled. It was an unprecedented situation after all.

"You can stay with me," Manu said. Tara didn't reply for several minutes. His offer had come out of the blue.

"My mother lives with me. You are welcome to stay with us if you are not averse to the idea. I think that is the only way out now."

"Would she like it?" Tara asked, clearly knowing how much Mary hated her.

"She will understand. I cannot leave you and Aryan stranded. I am not that heartless."

It made sense. Yet, how could she accept it? It seemed all wrong. She had wronged him and now he was going out of his way to help her.

"Let us check at a few more hotels," she said.

Again, Manu drove around on the water-logged roads until it was almost too dark and difficult to move around.

"I can't drive in this condition. Can't you see that the roads are waterlogged? The glass is foggy and the heavy rain is causing poor visibility. You will have to come with me, Tara. You don't have another choice."

He then cursed as he almost crashed into the bumper of the car in front of them.

Manu was speaking sense. It seemed potentially dangerous to drive in these conditions. Tara had no choice other than to accept his invitation. Her husband, the only other person who she wished would answer her calls, was still ignoring her. And so, she agreed.

As it turned out, his home was just a few blocks away from where they were then. Before they turned into his street lane, Manu called his mother to inform her. Curiously, all he said was that he was bringing along a friend.

Friend? Was she anything of that sort to him? Tara wished she could remain that at least.

5

Mary opened the door with a wide smile on her face. She hearted guests. Her face clouded the moment she recognized Tara. But when she saw Aryan, her face lit up once again.

"Who do we have here, Manu? Who is this little hero?"

Aryan beamed and Manu made the introductions. When he explained how they had ended up with him, Mary plastered a false smile on her face and welcomed Tara who smiled at her. She wanted to rage and rant but Manu would not perhaps like it.

How dare she smile at me? How am I going to stop lashing out at her? My son has not been the same ever since she had her way with him. I should probably throw her out into the flooded streets. That is what she deserves. She thought ruefully.

"Who is this Granny, uncle? Does she know stories?" Aryan asked Manu and Mary smiled.

"Yes, little sir. I do know. Do you like to hear them?"

"I love stories. My mother writes stories too. But it is only for big people. Not for kids."

Taking Aryan's hand, she ushered them all towards the couch and then went into the kitchen to make tea. After a few minutes, Tara entered the kitchen offering to help her. Anger bubbled inside her.

"Please go and sit in the living room. I don't like my guests entering my kitchen," Mary said without even looking in her direction.

Tara walked out of the kitchen perhaps embarrassed and hurt, whispering a hasty 'sorry'. Mary let out a snort of disgust and set about arranging biscuits and snacks on a plate.

"Manu... can you come here for a moment?" she called aloud.

When Manu entered, she asked him to take the tea and snacks to their guests.

"I prefer not to see her face much. Show her into the second guest room. And it would be better if she remains there the full time she is here. You may have forgiven her, I will never forgive her," she said.

"Mom, she will be gone as soon as the flights resume. Please don't create a scene."

"Don't expect me to be civil to her. I can't."

"As you wish," said Manu and walked out of the kitchen carrying the tea tray loaded with tea and snacks.

Mary couldn't understand him. How could he act so normal? She stealthily watched him interact with Tara and Aryan. With Aryan, he was talking merrily and urging him to eat. He hardly looked at Tara who appeared to be lost in thought. He appeared tense when she addressed him a few minutes later. Perhaps she had asked for directions to the washroom because he guided her to the common bathroom a few seconds later. Mary was sure he had not forgiven her. He was just being human by offering her shelter during a catastrophe.

After Tara left the living room, Mary watched fondly as Aryan interacted with Manu. Manu laughed aloud at something Aryan had said and she blinked away the tears that suddenly sprang to her eyes.

If fate had been different, Aryan would have been her grandson. She would have been a proud grandmother. Instead of hiding behind the curtains and watching him, she would have pampered him with homemade sweets and tons of love. And she would have loved her daughter-in-law too.

With a sigh, she returned to the kitchen muttering a prayer. She wanted clarity and peace of mind. She wanted the night to be over and Tara on her way to wherever she had come from.

After tea, Tara took Aryan into the guest bedroom allocated to them in the four-bedroom house, to rest and freshen up. Mary came out of the kitchen to ask Manu what he wanted for dinner. When he declared anything would do, she decided to make a four-course meal. She needed a distraction.

A little while later, Aryan burst into the kitchen, totally naked and rushed to her.

"I don't want the cream. Creams are for girls."

"Aryan, behave. You should not disturb aunty."

"Granny... I can call you Granny, right?" Mary felt a lump in her throat and swallowed. She would love to hear herself addressed that way.

"Yes, sweetheart. You can."

"Tell Mummy I don't want the cream. She listens to my other Granny," he said.

"Okay, if you don't want, I won't apply it. At least come and wear your clothes. Shame, shame," Tara said hastily. Aryan immediately rushed away from Mary and hid behind Tara.

Mary chuckled but turned away when Tara gazed at her with the remnants of a smile. She liked the kid but couldn't stand the mother.

When Manu returned after a bath, Mary set the dining table and invited them for dinner. She had prepared tomato soup, egg biriyani, raita, and salad, and kheer for dessert.

"Everything smells yummy. Thank you, Granny," said Aryan as soon as he sat down at the table.

Smiling, Mary began her usual mealtime prayer. Aryan leaned in and listened to her with his mouth wide open.

"I like that. My class teacher does the same. We eat lunch together," he said, once she finished the prayer.

"Is it? What is the name of your teacher?"

"Jasmine."

"Nice name. We should eat now, shouldn't we? And we shouldn't talk while we eat, right?"

"Oh, the same rule here too? She says the same."

When Mary nodded, Aryan turned to his plate and started eating the carrots from the salad that Tara had spooned onto his plate.

"I love carrots," he declared and grimaced when he remembered he shouldn't talk. He looked at Mary and mouthed, "Sorry."

"I love them too. Eat them fast or I might finish them all first!" Manu said.

Aryan stopped talking and munched on the carrots. All through this, Mary watched Tara. She didn't like how her gaze often flitted to Manu. Her son, even though he didn't seem to be looking at her, was completely aware of her every move. Once, Tara accidentally overturned a glass of water while she was serving some raita for Aryan. Manu immediately placed a napkin to stop the water from spreading. Whenever Tara reached out for something, he immediately served her. He was attuned to her every move.

Mary didn't like it. Not even one bit.

All the while, the rain continued to pour outside. The news channels were filled with alarming reports of how the flood was spreading throughout Chennai. People were being evacuated from low lying areas.

The area where they lived was on a comparatively higher plane. They even had power though many areas were reporting power outages. The entire five-storey building was owned by Mary. They had built it a few years ago after they had decided to settle in Chennai. They lived in the penthouse of the apartment.

The master bedroom occupied by Manu was only accessible via the spiral stairs in the living room. The guest bedroom where Tara was staying was next to the kitchen. Mary didn't want them to accidentally bump into each other as they showed in movies. Old flames had a way of rekindling via chance encounters. Even if the flames were still burning, she wanted to snuff them out before any irrevocable damage occurred. She'd had enough trouble the one time they had burned bright.

She prayed Tara had enough common sense to keep out of Manu's way. The boy clearly still pined for her. He was struggling to act nonchalant. If she had not been married, perhaps he would have begged her to return to his life.

Mary knew their story. She knew how sincerely and deeply Manu had loved her.

Five years ago

2010, Kannur

Mary was worried. How couldn't she be? Her only son had been whispering the name of a girl in his sleep, followed by a few words that gave her the exact idea of what he had been dreaming about. She was embarrassed but she had to ask him. What if he brought a girl home and declared that she was his wife? That they had married in court?

Her son's marriage was one of her most cherished dreams. She wanted to plan everything, starting from the flowers to the flavour of the wedding cake.

Of course, she didn't want to thrust the burden of an arranged marriage on her son. She wanted Manu to find true love. But she wanted to be involved in his story right from the beginning. She trusted her son, but the name uttered by her son had put her in a dilemma. Tara didn't sound like a Christian name. Although Christian girls these days went by all sorts of names, she wanted to be sure.

Mary waited for a chance to speak while he got ready for college.

Wasn't he fussing a bit more than usual about his looks?

As she watched, he discarded the shirt she had ironed and laid out on the bed. Rummaging through his cupboard, he took out and wore the new green T-shirt he had purchased the other day. He hummed a tune as he stood in front of the mirror combing his hair. Then after spraying a liberal amount of perfume into the air, he walked into the scented mist to absorb it. Then he swung left and right, pivoting on his toes to make sure he looked perfect.

He looked handsome, this son of hers. Manu stood tall in his six-foot frame, with wide, muscular shoulders. His chiselled face with a strong jawline was made innocent by his deep liquid brown eyes. Mary's chest swelled with pride.

Manu picked his backpack, gave her the customary peck on her cheeks, and hurried out of the house. When the sound of his bullet receded from their courtyard, Mary realized that engrossed in observing him, she had missed her chance to question him.

Her drunkard husband had left her a rich widow twenty years ago. Manu had been just three years old when he died. Her son had inherited the looks of his no-good father. But unlike him, he was intelligent, the genes she proudly considered to have originated from her.

Mary had been the district topper in her pre-university exams. Her parents had hurried and gotten her married the year she had turned eighteen when the marriage proposal from a rich man who had been charmed by Mary's beauty came their way. Her dreams of higher education had been swept away in the drunken dramas that occurred in her house daily. Also, her husband had wanted her pretty and made up, not chasing degrees or certificates only to be employed by some stranger.

"You will not have time for anything else, my dear. We are going to have plenty of kids," he had told her on their wedding night when she had tentatively told him about her dreams.

Even though he didn't leave her at peace any night, only one kid had come their way, their Manu. And she was thankful for that. He was her gem and he was living her dreams. He was in his second year of post-graduation in Zoology and planned to pursue a PhD after that. Was Tara his classmate? She would love her daughter-in-law to be well educated.

Throughout the day, Mary weaved different dreams all based on this discovery she had made. She had already listed the questions she needed to ask him. She wanted to meet the girl immediately if he was serious about her. He was a decent boy as far as she knew.

Many girls in their church group craned their necks to catch his eye during Sunday church. He had given the Sunday church a miss the last few months saying he had college stuff to complete. Now she knew what the stuff was.

Mary stealthily rummaged in his cupboards and drawers to check for any photos or letters. Nothing. Kids these days hardly printed out photos. They had everything stuffed into their phones. Even love letters. Manu had the latest iPhone and he never let it out of sight. Their communication might be happening via emails and Facebook.

What did she know about mobile phones or technology? Nothing. Manu had tried to teach her but her interest in such stuff was zilch. She was content with her landline and television for entertainment. She didn't want to become friends with strangers on Facebook. Some of those in her church gang were already warming up to this relatively new sensation.

Manu came back home at eight that evening. His final exams were commencing the next day. Mary considered whether it was prudent to question him about the girl. Shouldn't she wait for the exams to get over? But her patience ran out by the time he came down for dinner. He was armed with his phone and was busy typing on it.

"Stop typing and eat your food," she chided.

"Texting, Mom. That is the word for it. I am just messaging my friend."

"Is the friend male or female?"

Manu stopped typing and looked up at her.

"Mom..."

"So, it is a girl. Tell me, is it Tara?"

"Tara? How do you know about Tara? Are you spying on me?"

"I have not stooped to that level but I will if you don't tell me everything about her."

"I thought you might not be interested. But how do you know her?"

"You were calling out to her in your sleep," Mary blurted out after hesitating for a moment.

"In my sleep? Jeez! When? And, why were you in my room?"

"I came to open the curtains to let in some fresh air today morning. And there you were, shouting her name ..."

Manu grimaced and looked down at his plate. When he looked up, his face was all red. Was he blushing?

Mary stifled a chuckle and narrowed her eyes. Manu laughed aloud.

"I love her. She is the best thing that has happened to me. I want to marry her."

"Marry? Which church does she belong to? Did she pass the catechism test?"

"Mom, she is not a Christian. She is a Hindu."

Mary had expected this. Yet the confirmation did not ease her discomfort or erase her doubts.

"Lord, how can I tolerate this? How could you fall in love with a Hindu girl? You have now gone and destroyed all my dreams."

"Mom... don't be so impossible. You will love her too if you meet her."

"But..."

"Promise me you will be good to her. Only then, I will bring her here."

Mary fell silent thinking about all the possibilities.

That weekend, Manu brought Tara home. Mary had made the house-help shine her home from top to bottom. Then she prepared a sumptuous lunch. Both Tara and Manu were having their last exam that day and would have wished for a celebration. Manu had informed that Tara loved chicken. So, she took out her recipe book and prepared a variety of chicken dishes.

Mary watched as a shy but attractive girl stepped out of their car. Tara wasn't conventionally pretty. She had short hair, a slightly dusky complexion and was taller than most girls Mary knew. She had beautiful eyes, bud-like lips and a curvy body. She welcomed her into the house with a warm hug. Throughout lunch, she watched their interaction. Her son seemed besotted with the girl. His gaze never left Tara's but the girl was extremely nervous. Mary talked to both of them. She asked Tara about her family, about her studies.

"If you are not his classmate, how did you meet?" Mary asked when Tara said that she was a second-year postgraduate student of English literature.

"We met via the Nature Club in college. Both of us love nature." Manu answered for Tara.

Oh, so that explained the multiple Nature Club trips these past years. Her son loved nature. She knew that. But she hadn't known that it had also made him meet the love of his life. Their estates in Wayanad and Munnar had been his favourite holiday destinations from childhood.

"She is also part of the college music troupe where I am the lead guitarist. She sings beautifully," Manu said fondly.

"I would love to see you both perform together," said Mary.

They agreed to give her a private performance very soon.

Once the lunch was over, Tara helped her take the dishes to the kitchen. Her son, who never helped her in the kitchen, stood near his girlfriend laughing and helping her gather the plates. As though he did that every day!

"Do you realize what this relationship means to Manu? If he marries you, his church, his extended family, and possibly even his friends might ostracize him. Do you think it would be easy for you? Would your family agree?" she asked Tara when she finally got her alone.

"I don't know what the consequences would be for both of us. But I do know I cannot live without Manu. I can't even think of a life without him. Family, friends, and religion are all secondary. I value him more than anything else. My family might raise issues too. But if he is with me, I can face anything or anyone," said Tara.

"Would you convert to Christianity if I insist that is the only way you can be my daughter-in-law?"

"We have discussed this. Our love has been unconditional from the beginning. Manu loves me for who I am and says it is absurd to change the religion I was born and raised into to please him or vice versa. I agree with him on that. We will retain our faiths even after marriage."

Mary was impressed. His son had selected a strong woman. She was cool even during testing times. She beamed at Tara.

"So, when are you planning to become my daughter?

Tara sighed in relief and then blushed so deep that Mary laughed.

"We haven't decided on that," she said. Mary liked how she always used 'we' instead of 'I'.

"What? Hasn't he asked you to marry him yet? Manu! Manu, come here," she hollered until Manu dashed into the kitchen expecting the worst. "Go on... ask her. I like your girl. If you don't ask her now, I might have to reconsider my decision."

"Mom, you are impossible. I can't do it in front of you. Give us some privacy," he said and then dragged a stunned Tara upstairs to his room.

Mary finished washing the vessels and made lime tea for all by the time they returned. Their lips were unusually red and she knew the excess of spice in her curries had not caused it. It must have something to do with the excitement that made their eyes sparkle and the way they held on to each other's arms.

Tara came to her and asked whether she could call her Mom from then on. Mary beamed at her and gathered her in a hug. Anything for the happiness of her child and this was no sacrifice at all. She liked the girl and could understand why her boy had fallen in love with her.

Mary went to check on her estates in Wayanad the following week as she did every three months. Her undisclosed task was to tell her younger brother Isaac, who handled the affairs there, about Manu and Tara. She was relieved when her brother accepted the news calmly. He expressed happiness that Manu had found love.

"Nothing matters if the one you love is near you. I have seen you suffer all these years. I led a miserable life until Anna came into my life. Love makes everything beautiful. Tell him I approve."

Spending a week with Isaac and Anna rekindled her faith in love. Isaac and Anna had two lovely kids. An eleven-year-old son, Toby, and a seven-year-old daughter Cecily. Mary had never loved her spouse. At least, her Manu would.

When she returned home, she understood that Manu had brought Tara home when she was not around. Unlike the dishevelled state she expected, the house looked clean. Moreover, his wardrobe had become organized. She had long given up tidying up his things. He never kept anything back in place. He would randomly pull out clothes from a neat, orderly pile and destroy hours of her hard work in a minute. So, she had stopped caring.

This new girl in his life was making him change for the better. Even the kitchen smelled good. They might have cooked.

"Tara was here?"

"How did you know? Do you have a sixth sense?"

"I have a mother's sense. I think you should marry her soon. I like how she is changing you."

"Changing me? How do you think I have changed?"

"For one, your eyes sparkle with happiness. Being in love suits you. Besides, I can use some help in keeping your room clean," she declared.

When he laughed aloud and went out to meet a friend after kissing her on the cheeks, she didn't think that would be the last time she would see him laugh like that for a long while.

She never knew what exactly happened. But within a week, she couldn't walk out of the house without facing an insult of some sort. Snide remarks became common whenever she walked into the church. And Manu became a shadow of his previous self. He kept to his room and dark circles began to appear around his eyes.

It was her friend Susan who told her what had happened.

"Your Manu was caught on camera with a prostitute in a hotel lobby. A local newspaper published a story about it and somebody had also created a Facebook post. It created a ruckus. I didn't think Manu would take after his father."

Mary had listened, stunned. She couldn't believe it. Her son loved Tara. Susan had then shown her the pictures which she'd saved on her phone. The man in the photo was indeed Manu. The girl was hugging him in one picture. In another photo, she was kissing him on his lips. Mary was appalled.

That evening she confronted Manu.

"I heard what happened. How could you do that to Tara? I'm ashamed that you are my son. Are you proving you're your father's son?"

For several long moments, he remained silent.

"I have lost her, Mom. She believes it. As you do," he had muttered feebly.

The unshed tears glittering in his eyes were proof enough for Mary to believe that her son was innocent.

The days of self-torture that Manu afflicted on himself after that, made her wish that he had never met Tara. She had offered to act as a mediator but he had refused any help. He refused to explain what exactly had happened.

"It is too late. She hates me now."

Then she had decided. It was time to quit this place, which had become hell for her son.

7

When Manu woke up the next morning, the usual morning sounds were absent. Alarms didn't ring. There were no hurried footsteps or banging bathroom doors. Neither did the chimes of *pooja* bells or bhajans come from the apartment. Maybe, because of the floods, the tenants were taking the day off.

His office had declared a holiday today. The air-conditioner was off as there was no power. His mobile was running low on battery. He got up and connected it to a power bank.

Swinging his legs down from the bed, he sat up, stretched, and sighed. All of a sudden, a thousand visuals from the day before flashed before his eyes. Each one featured only one face: Tara. He had thought he had successfully forgotten her. Yet, the moment he had seen her in his house, all those forgotten desires had returned. Every fibre in him was longing to hold her in his arms. She had become prettier and more desirable than before. But it was a forbidden thought. She belonged to another man.

Tara had it all now. A kid, a loving husband and a promising career. He had moderated many book launches. But no other debut author had generated such genuine interest among the audience. Many of them claimed to be regular readers of her blog. Writing indeed was her forte.

Would she have become one if their paths had never diverged?

Even his life had turned out so different. Apart from his job at the online science portal, he was also a visiting professor at a university. He was a nonfiction author as well. Back in his youth, he had dreamed of becoming a wildlife biologist.

Manu opened the door to the terrace to begin his routine morning exercise. The outside view shocked him. The rain had flooded the areas surrounding their place. The entire floors of several buildings were underwater. There was no light shining from any of the windows.

He then looked down inside their apartment compound. It disturbed him when he saw small streams rushing down to the streets below. It would be just a matter of time before the flood water entered their locality. And the rains were still lashing heavily around.

The initial thought was one of despair. Then another thought brought a smug smile to his face. There was no way that Tara could go today. Or even tomorrow. The flood might take days to recede.

It was a selfish thought. Yet he didn't regret it. For the moment, they had nothing to worry about. Even if the floods worsened, because of the altitude of their locality, it would be impossible for the flood water to pose any danger to their building. They had enough food supplies as it was just yesterday morning that he had brought home their month's supply of groceries.

He desperately wanted some more time with Tara. In all probability, this would be the last time he would see her. He knew her. She would make sure their paths never crossed. He loved the kid too. It was impossible not to like him. Their presence in his house created a mirage that everything was fine in his world.

Walking down the stairs into the hall, he found Tara coming out of the kitchen. Their eyes met and he smiled. She had a glass of water in her hand. She appeared rattled by his sudden appearance.

"Aryan wanted water. He often asks for it around this time."

He didn't say anything but stepped aside to allow her to pass. He was standing right beside the door that led to her room.

Tara went in and closed the door. Almost on his face. It felt like a slap.

Manu walked into the living room and slumped into the couch. Sudden despair conquered him. He would never again be welcomed into her world. While here, she would create an invisible wall around her. New memories would slowly replace all the cherished memories they had once shared. A new Tara would replace the Tara who was once his very soul. She had her cosy little universe now. He had no place in it.

He switched on the data on his phone to get updated about the flood situation.

According to the newspapers, this was the worst flood situation faced by Tamil Nadu in the last 100 years. Thousands were left homeless. Many were starving. Voluntary agencies were trying to sort out the food and other medical needs of the stranded people. Many public buildings were housing displaced people. The opening of the sluice gates at the Porur, Poondi and Chembarambakkam lakes had further increased the flood levels.

Clicking on a given number, he called the person in charge of the NGO in his locality. The man inquired if they had enough food.

"Yes, we have enough supplies. We are not affected. I want to offer help in the rescue and relief operations," he said.

"Do you have space to accommodate some people? Our rescue centre is already crowded but people are still arriving," said the man.

"Yes, I can give accommodation to a few," he assured the man and disconnected the call.

Mary had risen and was listening to his words.

"What happened? To whom were you speaking?"

"Go out to the balcony and look what is happening around, Mom. Chennai is drowning."

Mary walked to the balcony and looked outside. Her jaw dropped open and she leaned on the door frame for support.

"What else can I expect when she has landed in our lives again?" Mary spat out.

"Mom..." Manu called out, a warning evident in his tone. "She is our guest. Don't speak like that about her."

"So, have you forgiven her for all the things she did to you?"

"What makes you think that?"

"I am your mother. I see how your eyes follow her everywhere. They are the eyes of a lover. You can't deny that."

"Mom, don't make assumptions. She is in this house only as my guest. I don't want to think about her in any other way," he lied. "And I won't allow you to make her life a living hell while she is here."

"Okay. Your wish. Don't expect me to be civil with her. I cannot fake a smile."

Mary exited the hall and entered the kitchen to cook breakfast. There was no power and the only thing she could make easily was *upma*. She busied herself cutting onion, chillies and carrots to add into the *upma*. She was still fuming when Manu entered the kitchen.

"Mom, I want to offer accommodation for a few people stranded because of the flood. We can, right?"

"Yes, we can. After all, we have already given refuge to the angel of death herself."

Manu turned away determined to avoid a verbal duel with his mother. He had to find a way to keep Mary away from Tara. Else, by the time Tara left their home, she would be nursing deep wounds inflicted by his mother's caustic words.

Tara's emotions were churning just like the floodwater raging outside. The words that the wind had carried to her ravaged her heart. Manu's smile earlier had comforted her. A few minutes later his mother's words had killed it. She shouldn't expect anything else. Her impulsive decisions had given birth to this chaos.

As usual, Aryan had gone back to sleep after drinking his customary glass of water. Lying near him, she gathered the blanket tightly around, wishing its warmth would kill the numbness inside her. Her dry eyes ached for a deluge of tears. She wanted to cry her heart out. Yet nothing came.

It felt strange to be under his roof and yet estranged from Manu. They had dreamed about a home like this and made plans to decorate their haven. The room felt as if it belonged in their dream. The pastel shades that dominated the furnishings had been her favourite. The modern artworks that tastefully adorned the walls were his. The empty space on the other side of the bed would have felt complete with his presence. And just at that thought, the dam of tears broke and raced out of her eyes.

The rain pattering on the window, leaving trails of silver threads shining in the morning light took her time travelling. They had first met on a similar damp, rainy day seven years ago.

Tara was then in the second year of her bachelor's degree in English literature. Manu was a senior studying for an MSc in Zoology, a rank hopeful for the entire college. Their worlds didn't usually converge. The science stream and the arts stream students belonged in parallel worlds that never collided. Yet it did for them, magically, amid the unorganized chaos of a bunch of teenagers trying to create music. Music had wiped out the prejudices that often kept the two streams apart. She was the lead singer and he was the lead guitarist in the college band.

Manu had initiated their conversations every time they met. He talked to everyone. She often forgot words in his presence, her tongue tangled.

Everything about him fascinated her. The light that animated his liquid brown eyes, lines that crinkled around his eyes when he laughed, his silky-smooth hair that fell lazily onto his forehead every time he moved his head. His broad shoulders made her want to rest her head on them. And when his fingers, long and soft, strummed the guitar, every cell in her body hummed.

It had felt like a meaningless crush until that college trip.

Tara had signed up for a trip organized by the Nature Club only because she knew Manu was the group leader. The trip had been to the interiors of the nearby forest reserve renowned for its rare species of flora and fauna. Her fascination for him did not go unnoticed by him for long. On the way to the reserve, his eyes had met hers often and she had found a question lingering in them.

Inside the reserve, while they were crossing a narrow bamboo bridge, she froze in the middle of the bridge, suddenly frightened and numbed by the chaotic vista of the wild stream that ran just metres below. Everyone else had crossed the stream without any incident. She had begun well, taking one step at a time. But she froze the moment she looked down and saw the white, frothy and raging stream below. After the initial encouraging shouts, all had fallen silent. The bridge was too narrow to accommodate two at the same time.

Then Manu had returned and encouraged her with kind words. Her fear had been replaced by a warmth she had never felt before. But it had not been enough to make her walk. Humiliating tears had streamed down her cheeks and he had wiped them wordlessly. Then, effortlessly, he had lifted her in his arms and walked to the bank.

Their friends had cheered for them. Neither one of them wanted to be near anyone else after that. Sometime that night, while they had sat around a raging bonfire, silently holding hands while the others sang and danced, she had opened her heart to him.

Tara had traced the four letters declaring her love on his palm, her tongue still unwilling to cooperate. He had squeezed her palm in acknowledgement and then traced a heart-shaped loop on her palm repeatedly. Each stroke sent delightful rushes of pleasure to every inch of her skin. He had taken her hands in his and kissed the tips of her fingers.

The same love that had left her tongue-tied, when finally expressed, had made her eloquent. She grinned, laughed at his jokes and talked nonstop. His arm snaked around her waist and held her near. She laid her head on his shoulders and breathed in his unique smell. They talked into the night sharing long-suppressed secrets and desires. After the embers of the bonfire had turned to ashes, they had parted reluctantly. The next day, the others had left them alone, and by the end of the trip, they had been declared a couple.

Very soon, she knew more about him than anyone else in the world. He could answer any question about her likes or dislikes. No other couple seemed single-mindedly obsessed with each other like them. Their affair was an open secret. And that had become the bane eventually.

But then, it had not mattered to them. All they had wanted were seconds, minutes and hours together, which presented only rarely to them given their different study streams. It didn't feel like a crime to bunk classes when one of them had a free hour.

They sought out the various deserted spots on the campus where he would pour his soul into her, with words and caresses. With his fingers roaming restlessly on her body, with every tug of his lips, every stroke of his tongue, he stripped bare her defences, making her aware of the demands of her own body like never before. The occasional Nature Club trips added fuel to the fire with long hours of togetherness in the lap of nature. Every day they fell a little more in love.

During his final year exams, Manu took her to his house. Mary had showered her with love. She had even demanded that they marry. They had fumbled with each other with feverish kisses and caresses and fell as a tangled mass of limbs and bodies onto his bed after he had asked her to marry him. If not for the presence of Mary downstairs, they would have spent the whole afternoon in each other's arms, crossing yet another barrier.

Her phone let out a beep declaring low battery disrupting her stream of thoughts. Fishing out her phone charger from her bag, she inserted it in the nearby plug and kept it on the nightstand. She realised there was no power. Aryan turned in his sleep and threw his right leg over hers as he snuggled closer. She kissed the top of his head and caressed his arms. She held him close and tried to end her mind's obsession with the man who now hated her. The man she had almost married.

Karthik, the man she had married, had not called or responded to her messages.

His behaviour puzzled her. What had she said yesterday that was so unforgivable? Wasn't he ignoring them more with every passing day? Didn't she deserve his presence on the most important day of her life?

Her whole life was a mess. Her relationships were all knotted up and messy. Some cords were now winding around her lungs and choking her.

Tara got up and sat on the bed hugging her legs. She rested her head on her knees and allowed herself to cry out her anguish. Every inch of her heart squeezed with pain. After tears rushed out, she finally found herself relaxing. She wiped away her tears and just then she felt a tug at her pyjama top. It was Aryan.

"Why are you crying, Mommy? I love you. Don't cry."

Suppressing an anguished sob, she pulled him near and whispered. "I was not crying. Dust got into my eyes. Don't worry, okay? Go back to sleep. It is not morning yet."

She hummed a lullaby and watched as he fell asleep again. She didn't need anyone or anything. Aryan was enough. He was her manna from heaven.

9

Aryan fell asleep again. After a quick bath, Tara changed into the kurta and leggings she had purchased the day before. The white floral kurta with blue orchids made her feel like an antique china vase. She also felt fragile as one. A harsh retort from Manu might break her forever.

She turned the knob of her bedroom door and walked out tentatively. And he was the first thing that met eyes. His figure was silhouetted against the door leading to the balcony. He turned as if he felt her eyes on him. Their eyes met and duelled for seconds. The tenderness that she found there took her back in time. Back to some secluded corner in their campus, their eyes locked in place, unadulterated love enveloping every cell of her being.

Unconsciously, her fingers moved to her throat to feel the pulse point, he loved to tease. The coldness of her wedding chain pierced her fingers.

In an instant, she remembered she was bound by several visible and invisible chains to another man. Manu's eyes hardened. His gaze also had focused on the shining golden chain and an angry red tinged his face. He strode out of the room. Her throat constricted and she swallowed. She would rather die than see him look at her like she was some loathsome creature. She followed him to the kitchen.

Mary glared at her when Tara entered the kitchen. The kitchen was twice the size of her tiny one in Bangalore. Yet, the presence of three people in the confined space made it feel like a narrow cloister. Especially as the other two hated her at sight. A tiny shiver of terror started at the base of her right calf. She pressed her right foot firmly on the ground to halt its progress.

For a long moment, Tara stared at the cut vegetables shaped like tiny cubes lying on the chopping board. She fidgeted with the hem of her kurta searching for words. Words that could shatter the wall of hostility that stood between her and the two individuals who had once been the most cherished people in her life.

"I apologise for what I did years ago. I cannot give any explanation as to why I did what I did. I request you both to forgive me if possible," she managed.

"Why are you asking my forgiveness? Beg for his forgiveness. He gave you his heart and you squished it ruthlessly. Before declaring him as the wronged one, did you give my son a chance to explain? How can you even show your shameless face to him?"

Mary's loud voice echoed through the house.

Tara wished for a hole to appear in the ground and suck her in. Tears pricked the back of her eyes. Blinking back her tears, she fixed her eyes on her feet, hunting for anything to say. But no words came out.

"Who are you shouting at, Granny? At Mommy? Don't make her cry. She already had dust in her eyes in the morning." A wide-eyed Aryan was standing at the door of the kitchen and giving her a puzzled look. Tara gasped.

"No. Granny was scolding me for not brushing my teeth. Have you brushed your teeth? Breakfast is almost ready. Come, come... let's brush our teeth together," Manu lied.

He came forward and caught Aryan by his arm. Aryan grinned and accompanied him after loudly asking Tara to give him his brush.

Tara looked up at Mary who had returned to chopping the carrots and onions with renewed energy. Knowing it would be futile to try and talk to her again, Tara left the kitchen.

After breakfast, Mary went straight to her room complaining of a headache. Aryan seemed to have become fascinated with the many books that lined the shelves in the living room. Manu took out a book titled 'Wonders of the Ocean' from the shelf and with Aryan seated on his lap, began leafing through its pages. Aryan's eyes widened with surprise and excitement as Manu talked about the various creatures that inhabited the depths of the ocean.

"I've seen many of these creatures on Octonauts. But they look so beautiful in these photos. Now I know what I want to be when I grow up. I want to become a marine biologist."

Tara involuntarily rolled her eyes remembering that just last week his ambition had been to become a fighter pilot. He had declared that after they had returned from the air-force museum.

"Great! You can keep the book with you then. Ask your mother to help you read it, okay? Some of the words might be difficult to understand."

"Oh, I know how to use the dictionary app on my iPad. I just have to type the word in the search box and click search. It will tell me the meaning."

"Aha! I didn't know that. You are so wise," said Manu, feigning ignorance. The encouragement led to a lengthy babble about his various study apps, his storybooks and his friends.

As if he felt her gaze on him, Manu looked up and their eyes met. The sorrow in Manu's eyes sent a dart of sadness that pierced her heart.

Tara retreated into her room to allow them to interact. Their proximity filled her heart with guilt. If God has chosen otherwise, she could have joined them.

While their happy voices reached her, her thoughts flew to those sultry days she had spent in Manu's home.

"Mom won't be at home for a few days. Will you come home?" Manu had asked while they were waiting to board the college bus. It had been an invitation that held so many promises.

By mere coincidence, their planned Nature Club trip had coincided with Mary's journey to Wayanad. Instead of going on the trip, she had left with Manu.

Tara had accepted his invitation fully knowing they would end up in bed. And they had. They had headed straight to his bedroom once they entered the house.

They had done nothing else other than make love the entire day. They pretty much repeated it over the next two days, living in the house as if they were already married. They cooked and never got tired of exploring each other. Then on the third day, knowing that Mary would return the next day, she had swept and cleaned the house. She had even organised Manu's wardrobe much to his amusement.

Two days later, things had taken a turn for the worse. The scandal and the photos had made her believe the worst. And she had thrown Manu out of her house when he came to meet her.

The truth had come out a month later. It had all been the creation of Ranjini, her own sister. She had sent the prostitute to pose for those photos. The woman had arrived at their house demanding full payment as Ranjini hadn't paid her. She had shouted out the truth for all to hear.

But by then, it had been too late. Manu had left Kannur. Days later, she found she was carrying Manu's child. She had wailed in the solitude of her room thinking about him, their child and their lost love.

When Karthik's mother had approached them with the marriage proposal a few days later, Tara had confessed the truth to Karthik. Instead of the rejection she had expected, he had told her he would raise the child as his own. It had seemed like her only choice. She was not ready to abort the child, she could never do that.

Tara had married Karthik within a week.

Could she ever tell Manu the truth? Did he deserve to know? Didn't Aryan deserve to know his father?

She had no answers.

A little while later, Tara wandered into the kitchen to drink some water. Manu was opening the cupboards and staring at them as though trying to decide what to cook. Sensing her presence, he turned to face her and addressed her.

"Mom is running a fever. What do you think will be better for her for lunch?"

"Oh, God! I will make some gruel for her. Maybe we can all eat that today. There is no power as well, right?"

"Yes. No power. The UPS still has some power left but I have switched it off. We will use it only in case of emergencies. The news says power might not be restored for another two or three days."

"What?!"

"Yes. Chennai is drowning. Unless the rain stops and the flood water recedes, even our building might get flooded in a few hours."

Maybe because he recognized the fear writ on her face, Manu came near and patted her shoulder.

"No need to panic. Rain is forecast for the next two days only. Hopefully, we can manage till then," he said.

"Yes, I hope so."

His nearness was doing weird things to her. Heat pooled in her belly and her heart raced. Tara turned away from Manu before he detected her thoughts.

She rummaged through the kitchen shelves to find the rice and other necessary items. Green gram and gruel might be the best for the situation. She measured two cups of rice and transferred them into a cooker. She found the green gram inside an adjacent drawer.

"Do you need my help?"

"No. I can manage. Can you keep Aryan engaged?"

Manu nodded and walked away. Was he disappointed? Or was it her wishful imagination?

Yet, within the short time she took to prepare the gruel and the green-gram curry, Manu and Aryan came in twice to check on her. Seeing them together brought warmth into her heart. They caught her humming a tune the second time they came in. The smile that curved Manu's lips reminded her of happy days long past. The enchantment of those memories spilt over into the present and made her gaze at Manu with longing. For a second, a familiar emotion, desire, flashed in his eyes and set her heart racing. But he quickly masked it and walked away again carrying Aryan on his shoulders.

Aryan seemed to be enjoying his new ride and she could hear his giggles now and then. When she set the dinner table, despair again clogged her heart. If fate had been different, her days would have looked exactly like this.

"He likes gruel? That is rare. I thought I was the only one who loved gruel. Atta boy," said Manu watching Aryan calmly eating the gruel with a spoon.

"He loves it. He developed a taste for it when he visited Kannur last year. Mother had prepared it for Father who was down with fever. And he insisted he wanted the same. Ever since then, he demands gruel every once in a while."

How would he react if he knew Aryan loved many of his other favourites as well? Often, Tara had found solace in the fact that God had given her a replica of Manu in the form of Aryan. Aryan had filled the hole in her heart, which had always sought Manu's presence and love.

"Tara, I think you should shift to my room. I want to be near Mom tonight. Often, her fever peaks in the morning. I will have to keep an eye on her." Manu said as he helped clear the dining table after lunch.

"Okay. We will shift."

Manu led them to his room an hour after lunch. He had changed the sheets and tidied up. After he left Tara alone to settle in, she gazed around the room. Aryan had tagged along with Manu. He was calling Manu's book collection a treasure. He hadn't finished going through them. Many of the books had animal pictures.

Tara lay on the bed and stared at the ceiling. The ceiling had stars and planets painted on them with fluorescent paint. At night, it would feel as if they were under the actual night sky. This was another one of their shared dreams. Tears pricked in her eyes and she bit her lips to stop herself from sobbing.

She pressed her face on the pillows and sighed. This was all she would have. These few days with Manu. Maybe she could amass many more bright memories in the coming days. Share Aryan with Manu. Make new memories together.

Yes, she would do that. She would gather these precious moments and cherish them forever. Maybe by the time they left, she'd have Manu back in her life as a good friend.

But could they remain just friends after the past they had shared?

It had to be that way. There could be no other future for them. Manu deserved someone better. He needn't know about her troubles. Some truths were better left undisclosed.

10

The clock on the wall struck nine jostling Manu out of his reverie. His thoughts were taking off in various directions. In the minutes after dinner, they had travelled at a breakneck speed into the foggy streets of the past and the brightly lit visuals of today. The result was turmoil inside his head. He was a total mess.

He could hear Tara hustling around in the kitchen. She had refused his offer to help clean up after dinner. His mother was still groggy from fever and had kept to her bed.

Aryan was the one keeping him engaged. Within a short period, he had grown fond of Aryan in a way he couldn't explain. What was it about the kid that strummed a deep chord inside his heart? Was it only because he was Tara's child? Or was it because he was seeing his unfulfilled dreams come to life with each sweet word uttered by the little bundle of energy?

Tara and he had woven dreams. They had dreamt of little boys and girls who might one day call them Daddy and Mommy. They had imagined how they would tire them out with their tantrums. The dream was raising its head now because Aryan was someone he would've proudly called his own.

The sounds from the kitchen ceased in a while. He heard Tara's footsteps approaching. Though he had his back to her, he sensed her presence in the room the minute she stepped into it. It had been always like this. It was as if his senses were extraordinarily attuned to her presence.

"Aryan, come on. It is already past your bedtime."

"Two more minutes, Mommy. This book has only a few more pages. Come here. I will show you the picture of a beluga whale that lives in the Arctic ocean. They are so cute."

"Beluga whales can wait. But kids should sleep on time. Do you remember what your ma'am said? Early to bed..." Tara paused and looked at Aryan expecting him to complete the saying.

"... early to rise, that makes a man healthy, wealthy and wise. But let's ignore her for now. She says lots of such stuff. Beluga whales are super cute."

Manu scoffed. Tara eyed Manu and shook her head in exasperation. He had never seen anyone, be it an adult or kid, so much interested in animals. He was a little genius and they would bond well. And the wish again returned with full force.

Why wasn't this kid his own? And with it came another thought. Why was this beautiful woman who haunted his dreams a stranger now?

He exhaled deeply and then ruffled Aryan's hair.

"Come on, hero! It's time that I showed you something that is even more exciting. You love the universe and the solar system, right?"

"Yes! How did you know?"

"I am good at guessing. Ready for some magic?" Manu asked. When Aryan nodded, Manu asked him to close his eyes. He scooped Aryan into his arms and climbed the stairs into his bedroom.

The room was in darkness when they entered it. Without switching on the light, Manu carried Aryan to the bed and laid him on the bed.

"Now open your eyes and see how Jupiter is hiding in that corner."

"Wow...this is so cool. Now, where is Mars, the red planet?"

"Just there. See...?" Manu pointed out Mars from among the various planets marked on the ceiling.

"I can't see it. Where is Mars? Show me."

Manu lay down right next to Aryan and showed him, Mars, by pointing in the right direction.

"It is so tiny."

"It is. Okay, now go to sleep. I will tell you some new secrets about Mars tomorrow morning. Good night."

"Can't you sleep near me tonight, Manu uncle? I want to hear those secrets now."

"I can't. Granny is not well, remember?" said Manu getting up from the bed.

"You can go away after I fall asleep. Just like my father does." Manu heard Tara gasp and his eyes darted toward her.

Was there an issue in Tara's life? She had turned pale and refused to meet his eyes.

"Enough, Aryan. Go to sleep like a good boy. Manu uncle must go to his mother."

"Just for five minutes, Mommy. Sing that song which always makes me sleep super-fast." Aryan pulled at Manu and made him lie down on the bed again. He then ordered Tara to lie down next to him too. Tara shook her head and instead sat near him on the bed.

"Okay. Sing, Mommy," Aryan ordered.

Manu held his breath, waiting for Tara to begin. He knew which song it was even before she sang the first note.

"Somewhere over the rainbow
Way up high
And the dreams that you dream of
Once in a lullaby..."

The song washed over him like a cool breeze on a warm summer night. She had sung this to him numerous times over the phone while in college. They had performed it together multiple times on stage. While she sang it, he accompanied her on the guitar.

Why had fate put them together if it was only to tear them apart?

Why had it played with their hearts? And why had it thrown them together again now?

"Lie down, Mommy. I want to hug you. Then only I can sleep." Aryan forced Tara, who was now perching on the edge of the bed, to lie down. He then made her turn towards him and hugged her after throwing his right leg over her hip.

Manu gazed at them and his heart longed to be a part of that cosy hug. The wish made him sigh deeply. Manu felt Tara's eyes on him and their eyes met. Her eyes were glazed with tears. He felt a stab of guilt. Was his proximity making her uncomfortable? He slowly tried to slip out of the bed when he felt a tiny hand pull him back.

"Don't go, Manu uncle. I need you to hug me now. Come on Mommy...sing. I promise, this time I will sleep."

Aryan turned towards Manu, put his hands across Manu's chest and threw a leg over his legs. His eyes were already drooping.

Tara launched into another lullaby and Manu tapped on Aryan's arms to the rhythm. Aryan's eyes closed soon and

Tara stopped singing. The next moment, Aryan raised his head and demanded another lullaby.

"You both should close your eyes as well. How can I sleep when you both are awake?" That was Aryan's next demand.

Manu obeyed him and closed his own eyes. Maybe it was the presence of the two or maybe it was Tara's song...he would never be able to tell what had lulled him into a deep, dreamless sleep soon.

He didn't know how many minutes had passed when a feeble sob woke him up. When he opened his eyes, Aryan was fast asleep and Tara was standing at the window, shaking from suppressed sobs. The rain pattering on the window sill was muffling her sobs. The dim light of the night light and the fluorescent stars drawn on the ceiling had silhouetted Tara against the window.

He wanted to go near her and wipe those tears. But that was not the right thing to do. This was not his place to be. He should just leave them alone. Perhaps his presence in the room was the cause of her distress.

Even as his sane brain ordered him to move away from her, an insane wish to resist it emerged. He didn't want to go away. Not yet. He hadn't felt this much peace in a long time. While he watched, Tara wiped off her tears and turned. Manu immediately closed his eyes. He didn't want her to realise that he had seen her cry.

He sensed her approach him. Perhaps she was gazing at him now. Tormenting minutes later, he felt the bed sag on his side. A mild fragrance of soap and her familiar, alluring scent enveloped him. His heartbeat quickened as he felt trembling fingers touch his chin. Manu forgot to breathe.

Tara ran her fingers along his jaw and then touched his hair softly. With each touch, years of yearning began to surface. Anger, regret and sadness began to melt away. Joy, which he couldn't resist, began bubbling up inside his cells. *His Tara, oh, how much he loved her!*

And when he thought he would burst with happiness; a cold drop fell onto his cheeks. A teardrop.

Manu's eyes flew open and Tara shot up from the bed and stepped away.

She was fleeing. He couldn't allow that. That single teardrop had allowed him to hope. Perhaps she still loved him. Maybe she was not somebody's wife entirely. He had to know.

Manu sat up and clutched her hands. Then at an infinitely slow pace, he pulled her towards him. He was ready to let her go if she showed even the slightest sign of resistance. With each delectable inch that closed between them, his heart drummed harder. He kept his eyes glued to her face, retracing the contours of each little detail on it that had kept him awake on many nights. Her dark eyelashes and her soft cheeks were wet with tears. Her lips were trembling with unspoken words.

"Tara..." he spoke her name gently as he tilted her chin up. She refused to meet his eyes.

He continued gazing at her fondly. When she looked straight into his eyes finally, they were swollen red and brimming with tears. And that broke his heart. The urge to comfort her became uncontrollable. He pulled her into an embrace and he held her tight while she sobbed her heart out on his shoulders. He leaned back on the headboard of the bed and combed her hair with his fingers. Her sobs still did not abate.

God, how much he missed her. The gaping hole inside his heart was spitting hot and cold like a blow-hole.

Any moment, Tara would ask him to leave, perhaps she would apologise for her lack of composure. Yet, he was not ready to consider it. He didn't want it to happen. He wanted her to return. To him. Back as his sweet nightingale whose songs made his days and nights brighter.

She wouldn't break his heart again, would she? It was going to be the strangest night ever.

11

Tara felt light like a feather. All the hurt, hidden inside her heart was slowly draining out. She clutched at Manu's shoulders and exhaled. Her tears had left wet patches on his shirt. His fingers caressing her hair and the soothing words he was whispering to her, everything felt like a dream. She didn't want this dream to end.

Her gaze flitted towards the bed. Aryan was now blissfully asleep. Guilt darted through her. She was a wife, a mother. She should put an end to this madness. Tara retracted her hands from Manu's shoulders and gently pushed herself away from him.

"Forgive me, Manu. This shouldn't have happened."

Manu refused to let her go.

"Don't, Tara. I have dreamed about this moment for years. Don't ask me to leave now. Can we pretend for a while that those terrible things never happened? That we never parted?"

"What good would that do to us?" Tara said, even as the dissuading voices from within echoed in her ears.

Manu crossed his arm and leaned back again on the bedpost.

"I don't know. But let's give us this one chance. We have met again because our story is still not over. I need closure. If you have forgotten me completely and moved on, tell me that. I have struggled all these years to forget you. I believed I had moved on. A glimpse of your smile and I am convinced that you still live inside here." Manu tapped on his chest. Averting his eyes, he got up and walked towards the windows. He stood bracing the window with his hands. Perhaps he didn't want her to witness his frustration and vulnerability.

Tara gazed at the man she still loved. She had found the pain that was crushing her heart, reflected in his eyes. Had the pain she had given him hollowed him out? What could she do?

A balance had been handed over to her. On one side stood Karthik, who had seen her through the darkest of times, and on the other stood Manu, the man who still owned her heart and whom she had wronged in a multitude of ways. The balance, without doubt, was tilting in Manu's favour.

Gathering courage, she took a step towards Manu. She wished she could kiss away all his pain.

As if he had sensed her movement, Manu turned around. He met her halfway through and pulled her into an embrace. Pulling back, he cupped her cheeks and then gently kissed her. Pleasure stirred inside her like a hellion and she kissed him back. He groaned as he deepened his kiss. He cradled her head in his hands and whispered words of endearment against her lips. The desperation in his voice and the feel of his hard body against hers felt like heaven. She wished she could drown in the heavy mist of passion that surrounded her.

But alas, she was a married woman. She shouldn't do this. Ashamed, she stepped out of Manu's arms.

"I can't do this to Karthik. He is a good man," Tara said, her voice strangled.

Manu searched her face and moved away from her. Yet when he turned towards the door, she realized, she didn't want him to walk away. Even if it was a sin, she desperately wanted this alone time with Manu that fate had dropped into her lap. The emotional upheaval of the day's events was making her head spin. Fighting her guilt, she called out to Manu.

"Stay with me for a while, Manu. Talk to me. Rage at me, scold me... but don't leave me alone. I am a mess right now. Help me."

Manu paused at the door for a long minute. Then slowly, he turned to face her.

"No, Tara. If I stay here for even one minute, I will want more than what you can give. I will want my old Tara back. It will be better if I leave."

His words tore at her heart. But he was right. They should stop this.

"Yes, you are right. Good night, Manu."

"Good night." Tara sat on the bed and dragged her fingers through her hair. And then when the sadness began to overpower her, she pressed her face into the pillows and cried bitter tears.

The tears lightened her heart to a great extent. After a while, she got up, put up pillows on both sides of Aryan and walked out of the room. She had to check on Manu. He didn't deserve what she was putting him through. She heard his voice coming from Mary's room.

When she reached there, Mary was lying on her side and vomiting next to the bed. Manu was rubbing her back and asking her to calm down. Seeing her enter the room, he stiffened for a minute. The next moment, he called out to her.

"Thank God you came. Her temperature suddenly peaked. Can you please fetch me a glass of water?"

Tara nodded and dashed to the kitchen. When she returned, Manu took the glass of water to Mary's lips and made her drink it. She was semi-conscious and still delirious because of the high temperature.

Tara went to the kitchen and returned armed with a few washcloths and an old bucket she found inside the kitchen balcony. While Manu tended to Mary, she quietly set about cleaning Mary's vomit. It was only when she was wiping the final few splotches that Manu noticed what she was doing.

"Tara, why are you doing this? Leave it. I will do it. Go back to Aryan. If he wakes up, he will be alarmed," said Manu.

" It's okay. I am almost done. Don't worry about Aryan. Once he sleeps, he wakes up only in the morning around three to drink a glass of water. He goes back to sleep again after that."

Tara emptied the bucket into the attached bathroom closet and returned with a wet piece of cloth and wiped the floor. After that, she sprayed disinfectant cleaner on the floor and wiped it off with a dry cloth. She soaked all the clothes in detergent and took them to the balcony deciding to tackle them in the morning.

She returned to the room and sat at the foot of the bed.

"Manu, her sari is wet with vomit and sweat. Shouldn't we change her?"

"Yes. We should. But..."

"Just get me a fresh sari. Or something light. We need to keep her cool. Perhaps a nightgown?"

"Let me check."

Manu returned with a nightgown after a few minutes and he held Mary in his arms while Tara changed the soiled sari. Mary stirred a few times and struggled a bit as if she didn't want them to change her clothes. Yet, she didn't have enough strength to protest. She went back to a deep sleep once they made her lie down again.

While Manu was tucking her to bed, Tara quietly slipped away. She didn't want to face Manu again.

Settling back into the bed, she hugged Aryan closer and exhaled deeply. Why had she met Manu again? Inside her mind, it was utter chaos.

As Manu confessed, she too needed closure. They had to move on. But now she was sure of one thing. She shouldn't tell Manu her secret. Manu valued family above everything else. If he knew Aryan was his son, he would never forgive her for keeping it hidden from him for so long. He might take him away from her. She couldn't even imagine parting from Aryan.

Tara lay listening to the sounds of the night. They slowly lulled her into a deep sleep.

She dreamt that floodwater had entered her room and Aryan was being dragged underwater. He was calling out to her and clutching at her hands. She pulled him with all her might, but she was losing her strength by the minute. With a scream, she woke up and sat upright on the bed. Wiping her face, she reached for Aryan who was sleeping peacefully at her side.

"Thank God, it was a nightmare," she muttered.

Sleep had vanished and she couldn't sleep anymore. She opened the balcony door and stepped into the balcony. It was still drizzling but dawn was near. Everywhere around all she could see was water. It was as if she was standing on top of a ship moored at sea. Many of the single-storied buildings that she had seen in the distance yesterday were now completely under water.

What happened to the people inside those buildings? Did they escape before the flood water entered their homes? Or had death stealthily entered in the form of a giant wave and captured them unaware in their sleep?

Tara shuddered at the thought. Dread enveloped her as raindrops began to fall again. The rain hadn't stopped ever since she had stepped out of the plane. Wasn't there an end to this horror?

Was her nightmare going to come true?

Tara quickly stepped back into her room and closed the balcony door.

Was nature trying to tell her that there was a God above watching her every move? Was it warning her to make amends for all her mistakes? Sweat beaded on her forehead and her palms felt clammy.

Perhaps she should tell Manu the truth. She shouldn't think about the consequences. As of now, nothing could be predicted. Manu deserved to know he had a son if the flood was going to win.

12

Mary's fever reduced by morning and she insisted that Manu go and get some sleep. After the kind of night that had passed, he hadn't expected he would fall asleep. But within minutes after he lay down on the hall couch, he dozed off.

The smell of *upma* wafting in from the kitchen woke him. Had Mary ventured into the kitchen? She should rest. He rushed into the kitchen to find Tara transferring freshly prepared gruel into a bowl.

"I was about to come and wake you up. You should make your mother eat this. I checked on her. Her temperature is normal now. A few hours of rest after a bowl of gruel and she will be back to normal."

Manu leaned against the kitchen door and watched her transfer the *upma* from another pot to a serving dish. He didn't know what to say to her. She was behaving as if whatever happened between them last night didn't matter. As if it didn't happen at all.

"I will prepare tea after you feed your mother. Let me go and check on Aryan."

Manu nodded and gazed at her retreating back when she climbed the stairs to the upstairs bedroom. Had he imagined all that had passed last night? He rubbed his chin with his palm and immediately remembered the soft feel of

Tara's lips. His dilemma didn't have a solution. Not only had he tasted the forbidden fruit, he now wanted to own it.

Shaking off his thoughts, he carried the bowl of gruel into Mary's room. His mother was usually a strong woman. She was hardly sick. But whenever she fell sick, she would become stubborn and difficult to handle like a two-year-old. Usually, he got her admitted to a hospital at the earliest. But given their situation, it was lucky that Tara was around.

"I am not an invalid. I can feed myself," Mary snapped at him when he insisted on feeding her.

While he watched her eat, he remembered the soaked clothes from the night before that needed to be washed. Inside the kitchen balcony, he found them all cleaned and hung to dry on the clothes rack. Even Mary's sari had been washed and spread out to dry.

Manu took a quick shower and returned to the smell of cardamom tea wafting in from the kitchen. As they had run out of milk, Tara had prepared black tea. Manu found the milk powder Mary had stashed for such emergencies and handed it to her.

"Use this if you want," Manu said.

"I like black tea more. Do you want me to add milk powder to your tea?"

"No, I don't like the taste of milk powder."

"I will use a bit for Aryan's tea. He wants his tea sweet and milky," Tara said.

Aryan greeted him with a hug when he came down after a while with Tara. Tara was maintaining distance from him at all times. Her nonchalance was frustrating him. He burned to gather her in his arms and kiss her. Everywhere. He longed to feel the softness of her skin yet again.

He exhaled deeply and forced himself to return to the painful present. Beside him, Aryan was talking about his school and friends while he ate the *upma*. He wondered aloud if his friends were missing him.

"Of course, they would be missing you. Do you miss them?" Manu asked.

Aryan pouted. "I do. We have music lessons every day. Our music sir plays the guitar and we all sing. It is so much fun."

"You know what? I have a guitar somewhere upstairs. Let me find it and I will teach you to play it. Would you like that?"

"Yes!" Aryan exclaimed.

After breakfast, Manu took the dishes to the kitchen and began cleaning them. Tara immediately came in and urged him to distract Aryan who was now insisting that he wanted to see his father.

"He didn't call?" Manu asked and Tara shook her head. She picked up the dishes and began attacking the dirty dishes as if they posed a grave danger to all of them. She refused to meet his eyes.

While he searched for his old guitar, many questions bothered him. What kind of a husband was Karthik? The whole world was aware of what was happening in Chennai. And still, he had not bothered to call. Tara was hiding something from him.

Manu found his old guitar in the loft and removed its dusty old cover. He hadn't touched it in years. The last time when he played it, he had Tara sitting next to him, fondly watching him play her favourite song. Today seemed like the perfect day to end its banishment from his life. Thankfully it seemed intact though it was out of tune.

He tuned it and played a few chords. Aryan's face lit up and he had a million questions about it. As kids were never allowed to touch their music sir's guitar, he touched it tentatively. Manu handed him the plectrum and asked him to strum. He did so and clapped his hands in glee. Manu then played 'Twinkle Twinkle Little Star' for him.

"Again. Again. Play it again," Aryan demanded. The next hour passed swiftly as he played more songs at Aryan's request.

They stopped only when Manu's NGO contact, Ramesh, called to ask if he could take in a few guests. A couple and an old man had arrived at their already overcrowded rescue shelter. Manu agreed and gave him his address.

A few minutes later, a motorboat arrived via the now flooded street carrying their guests. When Manu opened his door to welcome his new guests, his jaw dropped open. It was Rupa, Tara's friend from college accompanied by a young man and an old man he didn't recognize.

"Wow! The world is a short place. So, we meet again. And how!" Rupa's eyes widened when she recognised him. She exclaimed when she saw Tara.

Tara seemed overjoyed by the unexpected entry of her friend. It almost felt like old times.

"Manu, do you remember me?" Rupa asked.

"How can I forget you?" he said with a wide grin.

"Yes, I guess you cursed me a lot back then for being the old stick in the mud."

Manu laughed. Rupa quickly introduced her fiancé Pratheesh and her soon to be father-in-law Ramachandran to him. He invited them into his home and directed them to the living room.

"How did you end up in Chennai? The last time we talked, you were somewhere in Trivandrum about to be engaged to Pratheesh," asked Tara.

"I wanted to attend your book launch and my father-in-law had a meeting to attend in Chennai. So, we had left

Trivandrum two days ago by train. We got stuck due to rain and have been roaming ever since trying to find a proper way to get back to Bangalore."

"Good that we met," said Tara.

From the silent exchange that followed between them, Manu gathered that things were still the same between them. They were still thick friends. They used to share everything. Relief spread through him because now he had someone other than Tara to whom he could speak about the past.

By the time the flood receded, he wanted to make peace with his past. He wanted answers to every question that had kept him awake at night.

13

When Rupa insisted that she stay in Tara's room, nobody raised any objection. Except for Pratheesh who appeared a bit disappointed. Tara knew why she was insisting on staying with her. It was good that she was here. She could be her sounding board. She had lots to tell her.

Though they had talked frequently in the last few months, in the last few days, she had accumulated lots of heartaches that had to be drained off.

The minute Manu and Pratheesh walked out of their room, Rupa lowered her voice and addressed Tara.

"You have a lot to explain. How and where did you meet Manu? And what is the status quo now?"

Tara gave a sharp nod to indicate not to venture there and motioned towards Aryan who was jumping around with happiness seeing another familiar face. Rupa didn't seem pleased but she turned her attention to Aryan.

Rupa, who hadn't taken a proper bath in days, went to have a quick shower and returned wearing pyjamas. Seeing her thus reminded Tara of their college days when they lazed around in each other's homes trading gossip, secrets and jokes. How she wished she could turn back the needle of time. There were a hundred things in her past she wanted to do differently.

"How did this miracle happen? I thought I had lost my mind when I saw you both together."

"You are reading too much into this. Nothing has changed. It's worse than before. I am near him yet we are no better than mere strangers," Tara said.

"You are right. The way Manu looks at you tells me nothing has changed at all. He still looks at you as if you are his oxygen."

Tara swatted at Rupa.

"Tell me everything from the beginning. How did you two meet?"

As she knew Rupa wouldn't stop nagging till she heard everything, she told her how Manu had been the moderator at the book launch.

"I tell you, destiny has plans for you both. Else in this flood, when everyone is losing everything, how did you find each other? Oh my God, I am getting goosebumps." Rupa held Tara's palms and squeezed them.

Tara wished she could share her optimism. But there was absolutely no future for her and Manu. The sooner she stopped hoping, the lesser will be the heartache.

Tara dragged Rupa down to the kitchen as now they had to prepare dinner for everyone. Mary was still too weak. With three more people, the items Tara had cooked in the afternoon would no longer be sufficient. The power had not returned. As it might not get restored soon, they took out the stored meat and fish from the freezer.

"This fridge is so well stocked. I wonder how people who are in the habit of shopping for vegetables daily might be faring. My fridge has never been full till now. If a few extra guests come home, I will be doomed," said Rupa.

"My case is not different. We have a deli just below our apartment. I purchase fresh every day. But people like us won't stand a chance in case of a flood. We will go hungry from day one."

"Chennai is in a very bad state, Tara. I saw it firsthand. I had almost lost hope before those guys from the NGO found us at the bus station we were stranded at. We waded in waist-deep water to get to a safe place after we had gotten off the bus, carrying our luggage on our heads. We ditched half our luggage there and proceeded with only the bare minimum. The lines for food at the rescue shelter were long. What amazed me was even then was that they were going out to help others who were in similar or worse situations. Hats off to the many youth volunteers, including girls, who are pitching in with help from all sides. They are coordinating the rescue operation armed with their mobiles and laptops. Social media, which is usually the place for showing off or bragging, has turned into a help centre."

"If you were in the camp, how did you reach here?"

"It seems Manu knows the guy who rescued us. The rescue shelter was filled. The volunteers were asking locals who were in higher and safer places to take in new arrivals. Luckily for us, we were directed here. The situation seems bearable now with so many familiar faces around."

"I don't know how I would have survived if you hadn't arrived. Thank God for small mercies."

"Tell me. How is Karthik coping with all this?"

"I have no idea. He hasn't called me since the time I boarded the plane for Chennai. I called to tell him about being stranded here. But his phone is switched off. I tried calling him multiple times after that with the same result."

"But why? My family who is usually the least bothered about me called me multiple times while we were trying to save our phone battery. Are you both having any issues?"

"Not really. We had one of our fights before I left Bangalore. Actually, he was supposed to accompany us. He cancelled it at the last moment citing an emergency meeting at his office. I was furious. I don't even remember what I blurted out. Just that I acted like a raged cat. I even accused he was the reason for the state our marriage was in."

"What state is that? You said he is the best husband you could dream of. That he cared about you, understood you," Rupa said, narrowing her eyes.

Tara felt her cheeks grow warm with embarrassment. How could she tell her that she lived the life of a nun in that house? That she was more or less like Karthik's housemate than his wife?

"I was not lying. He is all that and more. But ..." Tara paused unable to continue.

Words were often not necessary when it came to friends. They read between the lines, heard the unspoken words and deciphered the true meaning of our words. Tara could see understanding dawning in Rupa's eyes.

"Tara, how can you live such a farce?"

"It won't be a farce anymore. He has given me an ultimatum. He called me when we were about to board the plane. He said he had waited enough. The Tara who would return to Bangalore should be his entirely. Body and soul. Not someone's ex-lover."

Rupa gasped. Her eyes grew wide with concern.

"Can you?"

"I have to. I had prepared myself to become the wife that he deserved. All through the plane journey, I was gathering arguments in his favour. How can I forget that he was the one who had been beside me when I was going through hell? He hadn't walked away when I needed support. Manu was nowhere around. But Karthik held my hands throughout. I was prepared to close the door to my past forever."

"You spent five years living under the same roof with that man who, I agree, has been kind and supportive to you. If you haven't fallen in love with him until now, I don't think you ever will. You can't force love. Love just happens."

"I have to try and make it work. At least for Aryan's sake."

"But why? Can't you give Manu another chance?"

Tara turned away to avoid answering that question. She washed the chicken pieces and began coating them with spices.

She wished they could have another chance at love again. In the last two days, she had fought with the familiar stirrings of her deeply buried dreams struggling to unravel and find wings. Her heart had fluttered like a caged bird and had sung about forgotten dreams.

"Isn't chicken soup a good remedy for fever?" Tara asked to change topics.

"I don't know. Answer me, Tara. I can't understand why you are acting like this."

"I have more than enough reasons."

"You should tell Manu." Rupa seemed adamant.

Before Tara could answer, Manu's voice sounded from the kitchen door.

"Are you hiding anything from me, Tara?"

Tara felt as if someone had pushed her off a cliff. How much did he hear? But the mischievous smile he sported told her she had nothing to worry about. He hadn't heard anything most probably.

"I was wondering if Mary aunty would like some chicken soup. It is supposed to be a good home remedy for fever."

"Great. She loves it," said Manu.

"Okay, I will call you when it's done. Did you want anything from the kitchen?"

"I had come to fill this jug with some hot water."

Tara took the jug from him. After rinsing it with cold water, she filled it with freshly boiled water.

"Manu, we might face a shortage of drinking water now that the water purifier is not working. Is the tap water potable?"

"During times like these, we have to be doubly careful. Maybe it's time we put into practice some of the survival techniques I write about on our website," said Manu.

With the power gone, the overhead tanks were running low on water. Manu, with help from Tara and Rupa, soon modified the tank lids using funnels and tubes to harness rainwater directly into the tanks.

Tara had read about the various survival techniques Manu was referring to. The Science Reporter had run a series about survival techniques after the 2011 Tsunami which had led to large-scale destruction and death. But at that time, she hadn't known that the man she was searching everywhere was the one behind the series.

"Aren't we lucky that we are stuck with a scientist during the floods? I remember the Nature Club trips where you used to find easy solutions to all kinds of problems," Rupa said.

The mention of those trips immediately brought in a set of pleasant memories and Tara's heart began to thud at her ribs. Manu's eyes held hers captive and she could feel that they were thinking about similar things. The butterflies that came alive in her tummy were proof that the inexplicable pull they exerted on each other remained strong. Her breath shortened and her cheeks burned as memories waltzed in one after the other.

Will she be able to return to Bangalore with her heart firmly back in place? The man who stood in front of her seemed to have no intention of returning her heart which had been his for years.

As he headed to his mother's room, Manu realized that he had interrupted a conversation that would have taken a more interesting turn if he had not barged into the kitchen. Tara was a bad liar but very good at hiding secrets. Even Ranjini had been unaware of their affair until their final year in college. She was hiding something from him.

Whatever it was, it would remain a secret unless she changed her mind. He knew it in his heart. The same way that he remembered tiny little details about her. He knew that she heaped her tea with two teaspoons of sugar. That she tilted her head to the side when she sang. That she had to cover herself from head to toe like a cocoon if she had to fall asleep. And she loved it when he kissed her nape. And...

Enough! He should stop dreaming.

What was it that Rupa wanted her to tell him? As far as he knew Rupa, she was very loyal. She wouldn't betray her friend.

Seeing that Mary was awake, Manu smiled at her, kept the water jug on her bedside table and turned to walk away. He had taken a few steps when he heard his mother call him.

"Manu, I heard voices. Has anyone else come into our home? What is the flood situation now?"

Manu explained that they had welcomed three more people into their home and that he knew one of them from college.

"Is there anything wrong? You seem worried?"

Before he could answer, his mobile phone rang. It was his friend, Ramesh, from the NGO.

"Manu, listen. A warning has been issued that water levels may rise by a few more feet tonight if the rain continues with the same intensity. It will be prudent if you evacuate the ground floor of your apartment. Water has already entered our premises."

"Okay. I will do that immediately."

A woman in her mid-fifties lived alone in one of the flats on the ground floor and the other was occupied by a married couple. He will have to inform them quickly.

He sat next to his mother and patted her cheeks. Her usually cheerful eyes asked him a hundred questions at once. They were asking for reassurance.

"Don't worry. Things will turn back to normalcy very soon. You shouldn't worry. Just rest. Okay?"

"Who called?"

"It was my friend Ramesh. He wants me to do some things urgently."

"No. You shouldn't go anywhere. I saw that the water has now entered our street."

"Mom, I am only going to the ground floor of our apartment. I have to warn them that by tonight the water levels in this area are bound to rise."

"Oh my God. Hurry. But remember that I have only you left in this world. Don't go out."

His mother's voice was barely a whisper.

"Mom! You are worrying needlessly. Okay, I promise. I won't go out of the building."

He made her lie down and then got up. He will have to inform the others. He might need their assistance if they had to evacuate the ground floor.

"We will help. It is the least we can do," Pratheesh and Ramachandran chorused when Manu told them about the situation.

Manu informed Tara and Rupa and quickly took the stairs to the ground floor. He knocked on the door of the married couple, Dhananjay Bhatt and his wife Soumya, while Pratheesh and Ramachandran went to the building lobby to examine the water level.

Dhananjay, the short, stout man whom Manu had first met when they had purchased the flat, opened the door. Worry was writ large on his face.

"Yes, Mr Manu. How can I help you?" he asked.

Manu quickly shared the information given by his friend. Dhananjay's face lost all colour. Soumya, his wife appeared at the door a few minutes later. Her husband turned to her to explain, but he could manage only a few unintelligible words. His wife was certainly made of sterner stuff. She patted her husband's shoulder and immediately turned to Manu for answers.

"Mrs Bhatt, you have to leave the house immediately. The water level in our area is rising rapidly and this floor might go under water within hours. Pack all your valuables, an emergency kit and your non-perishable food items. If you're okay with it, you can move into my flat as of now. If you want to move into any other flat in this building, we will help."

"Okay, Manu. We will come with you. Are there any precautions that we should take? If the house will be flooded, our electrical appliances might get damaged, right?"

"Yes. Carry your laptops and other small necessary items. Turn off the gas valves and move valuables to higher drawers in your cupboards. If the flooding is low, we might be able to save many items that way. And yes, don't forget your medicine kit if you have one."

Soumya nodded and vanished into the house. Dhananjay shook his head as if to clear his head and then rushed inside to help his wife pack.

Manu walked to the other flat on the floor and knocked. A young man opened the door. Though he seemed very familiar, Manu couldn't place him immediately. Manu's acquaintance Susheela aunty appeared by his side and she greeted him warmly.

"What a surprise, Manu. Come in, come in. Finally, I can introduce you to my wanderlust son. Meet my son, Varun Chinnappa."

The name sparked recognition. He knew the man. Varun Chinnappa was a YouTuber and travel blogger famous for his trips to the less-visited corners of the earth. He had contributed many articles to the Science Reporter.

"How wonderful to finally meet you in person. I am Manu Matthews. Senior editor at the Science Reporter. I didn't know you were Susheela aunty's son. She always talked about your wanderings. She never mentioned you were a blogger and Youtuber."

"Wow! After being regular correspondents for nearly a year, we finally meet. And during what times!"

"I know! But first things first, you will have to evacuate this house. Flood levels are rising in the area and it is feared that this floor might get submerged. I think you will know what to do. I have two other friends with me. You are welcome to stay at my place. But we will have to hurry."

Susheela aunty's mouth opened into a wide O. All the joy that had been shining in her eyes was now replaced by fear. Varun turned to his mom and gathered her in a tight hug.

"Don't panic, Amma. I am here, right? This too shall pass. Now show me what all we need to pack."

It took combined efforts from Manu and Varun to finally calm her down. Manu helped Varun pack his valuable camera, recording equipment, and precious data records. They carried them to Manu's study room, which would now have to serve as another bedroom. Varun suggested they move his backpacking items including his sleeping bag.

"We can shift the folding mattress and bed I purchased when I came this time. I usually don't stay for more than a few days but my next project is going to be very near Chennai. It is time I spent some quality time with Amma," said Varun as they moved the couch in the room to one corner. Manu moved around his books on his shelf and made space for Varun's CDs and various electronic equipment.

When they returned to Varun's flat, Susheela aunty was busy in the kitchen. She was transferring the food she had prepared into containers. Her stash of spice powders, grains and grams in big pet jars were all taken out from the cabinets as if she intended to take them all with her.

"Amma, we cannot take all those. You will have to leave them here."

"No way. You don't understand kitchen stuff. If I am right, Manu is hosting others in his house along with us. We will have to preserve all the food stuff. God knows when things will return to normal. I suggest we move our extra cylinder and gas stove as well to your place."

She was indeed wise. Manu didn't think their stack of supplies would be enough to last another few days with more members joining in. And they had only a few hours left before the flood waters crossed over into their compound. He had gone to the outer compound wall along with Varun to check.

With some additional help from Pratheesh and Ramachandran who were helping the Bhatt couple to move to Manu's room, they finally transferred Susheela aunty's kitchen treasures. She didn't seem much worried about her other valuables as much as she was about her kitchen treasures. She had even packed a dozen ceramic plates, cups and spoons saying they might need them.

Her wardrobe, which was filled with costly sarees, just got a cursory glance from her. But she packed all her best bed sheets and blankets and bath towels saying someone might need them. All her nighties and casual wear sarees also got equal attention. When they tried to dissuade her from packing them, she scolded them, saying they didn't know what really mattered.

"Food, clothing, shelter... that is the order in which we should value things. Without food, nobody can survive. Clothes are essential as they protect us from harsh climates. A shelter is the least reliable of the three. See what happened to us now. I had always thought of this house as the safest place on earth. And see it now. When a stack of papers declares a piece of earth or building as ours, we think it will remain ours forever. There is no forever. We are all fools if we believed that. What is mine today might become yours tomorrow. Who knows what God has written in our destiny," Susheela aunty lectured them as they climbed the stairs loaded with her kitchen treasures.

His mother had often referred to Susheela aunty as a wise woman. She had allowed her son to chase his dreams and hadn't chained him to herself as many widows tended to do. Though she had retired as a school headmistress a few years ago, she still took out time to tutor underprivileged children who showed promise. She was even sponsoring the education of some of the kids of her maids.

Manu smiled to himself as he led her into his study. Susheela aunty's presence in the house would surely be a boost of positivity for all of them.

Susheela aunty headed directly to meet his mother when she learned that she was down with a fever. A few minutes later, their laughing voices sounded from the room.

The Bhatts were not his acquaintances though Mary was on friendly terms with Soumya. Dhananjay usually kept to himself. They were both software engineers at an MNC based in Chennai.

When he pulled out his phone to call his friend Ramesh for the latest updates, his phone battery died unceremoniously. When Varun saw his frustration, he quickly handed him a power bank.

"As I travel long and wide for my work, mostly to places without electricity, I have multiple power banks with varied storage capacity."

The news that he received from his friend was not something they could find relief in. The death toll was rising and people were still stranded in remote areas. Food was becoming scarce. Drinking water shortage was the biggest problem. Even though the water was everywhere, in some areas people were forced to drink polluted water leading to the spread of water-borne diseases.

Tara came searching for him along with Rupa. The amount of drinking water they had won't be sufficient. With more members being added, their stock would probably last a few more hours only.

"Don't worry. It is still raining nonstop. We will harness rainwater."

Then an idea struck him. He knew he had to help the others stuck elsewhere as well. If people could access social media, perhaps he could spread the know-how.

"Varun, are you up for some charity work? This will surely go viral."

"Viral? You had me at that. Tell me what to do," said Varun.

Manu sent Tara and Rupa to find some clean buckets. Rummaging through his loft, he found a piece of tarpaulin, which he had purchased long ago.

"I know what my video is going to be about. You are going to teach my viewers how to create a rain-catcher, aren't you?" said Varun.

"Yes. You got it right."

"Good idea, pal. Let's do it. It will be more informative if we include how to easily sterilize the drinking water as well."

"Right. Let's create your soon-to-be-viral video."

Varun fist-bumped Manu and then set about transferring his recording instruments to the roofing shed on the terrace which housed Mary's kitchen garden.

15

Tara had seen many of Varun's YouTube videos. His style was to engage people with his unique content. More than quantity, he focused on quality. His viewers loved his videos for the same reason. He was in his mid-twenties and already he was one of the world's top travel bloggers.

From what she had learned from Susheela aunty, he had packed a backpack and left to explore the world. A few fellow wanderlust guys had accompanied him just after graduating from high school. Though she had her apprehensions, Susheela aunty had decided not to clip his wings. Before long, he was earning from his passion. And he was always in touch with her no matter which corner of the earth he was currently in.

Aryan, who had become doubly excited ever since the camera was set up, was shooting question after question to Varun. Varun, his new hero, had finished setting up his camera in one corner of the shed where he had enough light to shoot.

After multiple trials, Varun was ready. He had recruited Tara to help. Rupa and Susheela aunty had taken over the kitchen. Meanwhile, Manu was in another corner of the shed. He was making something using PVC pipes and a tarpaulin sheet.

"Can I borrow your kiddo? I think I need a co-anchor today," Varun enquired while he made tiny adjustments to his video camera. He had made Aryan sit on a chair to focus his camera and to check the lighting.

It would be twilight soon. If Aryan created any problem, his shooting will be jeopardized.

"Do you want to take that risk?" Tara asked.

"Please, please, Mummy. I will not trouble him." Aryan who had heard Tara, promised solemnly. Tara raised her thumb in approval when Varun vouched for Aryan. Varun joined Aryan on the chair.

"Just press the record button when we are ready. At the count of three. Here we go... One, two, three."

Tara pressed the record button and Varun began.

"Dear friends, how are you all doing today? Do you wonder where I am today and why I have this smart kid with me? I am in Chennai. Yes, guys, you heard it right. Chennai is facing the worst flood situation in decades. We all need your prayers and support to get out of this situation safe and sound.

An hour ago, water entered my flat and I have taken refuge on the top floor of our building. As of now, we are safe. We do not lack any basic amenities. But since we are facing a power outage, we are facing a shortage of safe drinking water. I know many others in Chennai are facing the same situation currently.

My host here, Mr Manu Mathew, a senior research scientist and editor with the popular science portal sciencereporter.com, has come up with the perfect solution. He will show us how we can construct a rain catcher easily."

As instructed earlier, Tara paused the recording. Varun asked Manu to join Aryan, while he went to check the previous recording and set up the camera for a longer shot.

After adjusting the camera angle, he joined Manu and Aryan. All the required items had been arranged on a table on which the camera was now zooming in. Manu began on cue.

"Rainwater is water in its purest form, especially during a flood. At a time like this, a rain catcher can save lives. To create an efficient rain catcher, these are the things we need. A piece of tarpaulin or non-toxic plastic sheet, PVC pipes and a thread. We also need four pieces of pipes or poles. Two long ones of uniform length like the ones Varun is holding and two short ones like the ones with Aryan. Now we will create a tiny shed with this by tying the tarpaulin to the pipes."

Manu tied the pieces of the pipes to the tarpaulin sheet and then fixed the pipes into four flowerpots. After that, he adjusted the pieces in such a way that the long pipes were at the back and the two small ones were in the front. He kept a bucket at the lower end and then used the water spray to simulate rain falling on the sheet. Water began to run down the tarpaulin sheet due to its slope and collected in the bucket.

Again, at Varun's cue, Tara stopped the recording.

Moving on, Manu kept the contraption on the terrace where the rain was still pouring heavily. After capturing pictures of the rain catcher in its natural setup, Varun again set up the camera to focus on the chair they had occupied at the beginning of the shoot. Aryan sat there with a very content smile and they together began the countdown to record.

"So, guys, we hope this video will help you to solve your current drinking water problems. We have another important tip from Mr Manu to share with you. Even if you have a drinking water supply line, it might have got polluted en route because of the flood. To ensure the water is entirely safe, pressure cook the water using your ordinary pressure cooker for fifteen minutes. Almost all disease-causing bacteria and viruses die when subjected to high temperatures under pressure.

We are signing off with prayers for all those who are caught in worse situations now. Feel free to download this video and share it with those in need. Peace and Love."

And with that, they were done.

After fist-bumping Aryan, Varun vanished into the study to finish editing the video and uploading it on his YouTube channel.

Aryan who wanted to follow him was quickly whisked off by Manu to the living room where they picked up their guitar lessons again.

Tara returned to the kitchen to find Soumya, Rupa and Susheela aunty huddled together on low wooden stools. They were discussing the floods. Soumya and Susheela aunty were worried about the extent of the damages they would face. After all, their flats were currently under water. Susheela aunty seemed to have resigned to the fact that they would lose most of their life's earnings in the form of electronics, furniture and clothes.

Soumya was shedding tears of despair. Her husband had taken it worse. He had gone down to check the water level and had found their entire floor submerged. He had retreated to the room that had been allocated to them immediately and was grieving quietly. They had purchased the flat a year ago and had lovingly decorated everything.

"A house of our own had been our most cherished dream. As we both love to travel, we bought memorabilia from places we visited, to remind us of those trips. Those tiny treasures transformed the house we purchased into our nest, our home. And now everything is gone." Soumya sobbed.

"Daughter, don't get attached to material things. They don't last forever and can be easily replaced. Now, wipe your tears and give this black tea to your husband. Cheer him up. We will face it together."

Soumya got up and left the kitchen with the glass of sugarless black tea requested by her husband.

Tara took tea to Manu, Pratheesh, Varun and Ramachandran who had gathered now in the living room. Varun's video was going viral as predicted.

Aryan had fallen asleep on Manu's shoulders and she picked him up and went to their bedroom to tuck him into bed. While coming down, she heard Soumya's panicked cries.

"Somebody help. My husband... we were just talking and then suddenly he began having chest pain..." When Tara reached the room, Dhananjay was clutching his chest and was drenched in sweat. Ramachandran, who was a former nurse, quickly enquired to Soumya if Dhananjay was allergic to aspirin. When Soumya shook her head, he took out an aspirin from his wallet. He always kept a few aspirins in his wallet as he was also a heart patient.

"Chew this, Dhananjay, it will save you. Manu, call an ambulance. We have to transfer him to a hospital as soon as possible." While Dhananjay chewed on the aspirin even as he battled with his pain, Ramachandran, made him rest on the bed in a half-sitting position, with his head and shoulders well supported with pillows and knees bent to ease the strain on the heart. Next, he loosened his clothing at the neck, chest, and waist.

As Soumya continued to wail, Rupa led her out of the room. Tara joined them.

"Soumya, you need to calm down. Did Dhananjay have any heart problems? The doctors will need his medical records on hand to hasten the treatment. You are a brave girl. Pull yourself together. He needs you now," said Tara.

Tara's words had an immediate effect on Soumya. Wiping her tears, she went back into the room and found the file that had his medical records.

Dhananjay had been ignoring a high cholesterol problem for months. He hardly exercised and his desk job as a techie didn't help either. The stress caused by the loss of their home had taken a toll on him.

With each passing minute, Dhananjay's condition worsened. How were they going to find an ambulance for him when every single road and street was flooded? Even air ambulances worked rarely after sunset because of visibility issues.

Was Dhananjay going to end up as another casualty of these devastating floods? Tara sent prayers to heaven to dispatch a miracle their way.

16

"We are facing an emergency here, Ramesh. One of my tenants had a heart attack minutes ago. We need to get him to a hospital immediately," Manu explained. The call had taken forever to connect as Ramesh's number remained continuously engaged.

"Share your location details and the rescue team will be there as soon as possible," said Ramesh once Manu explained all details about their situation.

After disconnecting the call, he explained to Varun, Ramachandran, Pratheesh and the women that they will have to take Dhananjay to a first-floor balcony from where it would be easier to access the ambulance boat that would come in. It was a herculean effort but it had to be done. He went from door to door asking if any of them had a wheelchair. Luckily, he found one in a third floor flat. The wheelchair had been used by the late mother of the flat owner. They had kept it in her memory.

It took them a little more than half an hour to get Dhananjay down to the first-floor balcony facing the road.

While they were waiting for the boat, the women went from door to door to all the flats in the apartment asking if they had an emergency medical situation that needed immediate attention. They didn't want to take any chance.

To their relief, they were all safe and didn't have any problem except a shortage of stored drinking water. That issue too was being sorted out thanks to Varun's video which was now being shared everywhere via WhatsApp. As many of them were employed and commuted for hours daily to work, they had multiple power banks.

A boat ambulance arrived soon, a fishing boat specially modified into an ambulance. Manu and Varun had been worried as to how they will transfer Dhananjay to the boat as the receding flood water level had reached a few feet lower than the first floor by then. But the rescue personnel were prepared with safety harnesses and pulleys.

Dhananjay was lowered into the boat after being secured safely in the wheelchair. He was immediately attended to by the waiting medical team inside the boat. Soumya who was overcome with grief was allowed to join the party and Manu jumped in with her as a helper.

Their destination was the Military Hospital at St Thomas Mount which had been made functional. Treatment was being given to many flood-affected patients. The vista on the way was unbelievable. Never had he witnessed such destruction. It was as if nature was at war with humanity. Every single street that he knew like the back of his hand now looked like a ghost of its former self. Trees, vehicles, vessels and other junk floated and were being carried around by the flood water.

Rescue volunteers were everywhere. Even in the darkness, they were moving around in small boats asking if anyone needed help. Once they reached the hospital, Dhananjay was shifted into the ICU and preparations were on for an angioplasty.

While they waited, they talked.

"If something happens to him, I won't survive. I don't know how to live if something happens to him." Soumya sobbed.

"He is going to be okay. Do you hear me? You need to be strong enough to take care of him once he returns home. You look as if a cup of coffee would do you good. Sit right here, I will bring you a cup of coffee. Is that okay"

"Okay," Soumya said, trying very hard to smile.

When Manu returned after a while Soumya appeared to have fallen asleep. But when she failed to respond to his calls, he called the duty nurse to check on her. She was taken to the emergency room and attended to by the general surgeon in charge.

"It is probably just stress. We are doing a few other tests."

Manu walked toward the waiting area and sat on a chair. Running his hands through his hair, he thought about the people who were now at his home. They would be anxious about what was happening here. He called Tara but the call didn't go through. He called Varun. His phone was busy.

Manu walked along the corridor to clear his mind. A wail sounded further in the corridor. A youth who had been buried under a collapsed building during rescue operations had just been declared dead. After offering his condolences, he walked a bit further.

A middle-aged male nurse, who was wheeling a patient to his room, greeted him.

"Testing times. I hope your loved ones are safe."

"Yes, they are." Manu stepped in and joined him in pushing the gurney.

"I can't imagine why God is making us go through all this. Every other moment, I am hearing about another death or trauma. Won't this ever end?"

"Yes. It will. Every night is always followed by dawn."

"You are right. Talking about good things, the pregnant lady whom they airlifted in the afternoon delivered a baby boy. They have named him Sreyas in honour of the pilot of the plane that rescued her."

"That is an uplifting piece of news indeed."

"What this flood has taught me is that there is no guarantee to our lives. We will be gone any second like a wisp of smoke. Live like there is no tomorrow. Take risks, make the right choices and never get anything get in between you and your loved ones. In the end, when you die, they are the ones who will shed a few tears."

They had reached the room of the patient and the nurse took charge of the gurney.

Manu turned back and returned to the waiting area. He went into the reception to enquire about the two patients he was in charge of.

"We have good news for you. The angioplasty was successful. Your friend is out of danger. Mrs Dhananjay is also perfectly fine. In fact, congratulations are in order. She is pregnant." The nurse beamed.

Manu's face lit up with a smile. He dialled Varun. The call didn't connect again. Someone tapped his shoulders. It was a youth who looked like he hadn't slept in days.

"Can I borrow your phone? Mine just ran out of charge."

Manu handed over his phone. The youth sat near him and while he spoke to whoever it was at the other end, Manu understood that he was one of the many rescue volunteers he had seen on the way to the hospital.

The youth returned the phone after a minute and thanked Manu.

"I should thank you. If not for the dedicated work volunteers like you are doing, my friend, who is now out of danger, would now be dead."

"Your friend is one of the lucky few. Many are dying because we reach too late. Many areas are still inaccessible. We need more volunteers. We need more connectivity."

"Can I have the number of your group? Maybe I can chip in with a bit of help after I return home."

"The number I called now is that of the landline at the place we are using as our workstation. I am Raghu, a techie basically and we have formed a crisis management team to coordinate the various rescue operations. We could use some help."

"I am Manu. I am a scientist and editor at the web portal sciencereporter.com."

"Okay. I was wondering why you seemed familiar. You are the guy who taught us how to make rain catchers. I can personally say it has helped thousands. We need more of such videos. A flood will have aftermaths like epidemics. We need to make people aware of them. You and Varun should team up again and help us."

"Sure. I will contact you once I return home. I will ask Varun and let you know. I am sure he will help. His social media outreach made the video go viral so fast."

"That is great. Come, we will discuss it over dinner. There is a kiosk set up here to cater to the needs of carers like us."

Manu soon learned that Raghu's own family was stranded in their village, on the outskirts of the city, but safe. Their stash of food and medicines was, however, low.

"Thousands who are facing similar situations. Food and other essential items are being donated by people from all over India and reaching Chennai. But we aren't able to make them reach the needy at the required time. Organization and coordination of the collection and dispersal in itself is a big task. We are at it day and night but handling such a calamity requires all the help that we can receive."

By the time they finished their dinner, Manu was determined to help. Chennai was his home, and it was time to step in and give back the goodness and love the place had bestowed upon him.

17

Dinner was a quiet affair that evening. Even while they were putting the dishes away after cleaning them, Susheela aunty who was usually bubbly and talkative was silently shedding tears. She shared a close bond with Dhananjay and Soumya.

"Aunty, all we can do is pray. I am sure Dhananjay will be back among us soon."

"That kid was like my own son. They bring me a gift whenever they return from one of their trips. There isn't another kid who has such goodness inside his heart. First, his home was flooded and now this. Why is God testing him?"

"Think about it this way aunty. Because he was here, there were so many around him to help. I think the first aid given by Ramachandran uncle helped. Imagine if that happened when they were alone at home. Soumya would have panicked and it would have become worse. I hope we were able to get him to the hospital in time," said Tara.

"I agree. But until I hear he is safe, I won't be able to find peace," said Susheela aunty.

Susheela aunty had served Mary dinner before they started eating. Once the dishes were done, Rupa and Susheela went to Mary's room to check on her. Tara returned to her bedroom to wake up Aryan who hadn't had dinner. The excitements of the day had made him tired. Rupa joined Tara a few minutes later.

"We need to do something to cheer up the others. Susheela aunty will make herself sick if she continues worrying this way."

"Let me gather everyone in the living room. We have to distract her and the others. We have to find a way."

"Okay, I will give Aryan food, make him sleep and then join you all in the living room."

When she joined them, Ramachandran was talking about how stories heal.

"I know the power of stories. They heal. I think the incident with Dhananjay today reminded us all in some way about loss. At least it did for me. I know Tara is a writer. Varun is a traveller. Why don't we share one story each? It can be a story of someone you know or a story from your own life. The only condition is that it has to be one of hope. What say?" Ramachandran asked.

"That is an excellent idea. But who will start?" said Varun. Ramachandran volunteered to be the first storyteller.

"I will set the ball rolling. Okay, this is a story from my own life. I have never talked about this to anyone. But today, I think I need to tell this story. My late wife Sunanda, and I were college sweethearts. She was pretty, kind and the most caring person I ever knew. She became pregnant with Pratheesh in the third year of our marriage. It was the happiest nine months of our life.

We eagerly waited for the day when we would finally become three. We painted the nursery, bought baby clothes and debated over the best name for him. She had no complications during the delivery. We were so happy. Then suddenly on the second day, she started haemorrhaging.

The bleeding wouldn't stop. I lost her within a few hours. I was heartbroken. I didn't want to live. She had been my anchor, my home and suddenly I had nowhere to go. I had been an only son. There were no siblings with whom I could share my grief.

Sunanda's mother had come to be with her to take care of her and our child after delivery. I began to look at the child as someone who had been the cause of her death. I avoided looking at the kid for weeks. I left the house if I heard his cry. I was deep in depression.

Then came the naming ceremony when my mother-in-law forced me to sit with the child on my lap. He was fast asleep as if he thought he was safest on my lap. All the time, I was fighting the urge to toss the child away and run. And then he smiled in sleep, and two cute dimples appeared on his cheeks. Exactly like the ones of his mother.

I burst out into tears the next moment and my healing began. Sunanda had given me the best gift a woman could give her husband and I had thoughtlessly ignored it all. I named him Pratheesh, which meant hope. I spent my days finding ways to make him smile, to glimpse the dimples that had become so dear to me. I love people who make him smile. I love the things that make him smile." Ramachandran choked on the last words and fell silent.

Pratheesh, who was visibly struggling with his emotions, got up from his chair and hugged his father. Rupa turned away to blink away her tears. Tara squeezed her hand to reassure her.

"Okay, my intention was not to make anyone cry. But thank you for giving me this moment. Who will go next?"

Pratheesh raised his hand.

"My father told you the story of him and my mother. A story I would not have perhaps heard if not for today.

Maybe I should tell a tale that will lighten the mood a bit.

A few months ago, on September 23rd to be exact, I was attending this conference of artists and art moguls in Bangalore. We wanted to represent someone who was a traditional Kerala mural artist. The only artist who had shown up was far from traditional and was selling trash in the name of Kerala mural art.

But we didn't have much of a choice. So, we decided to go ahead with the artist. When I entered the elevator a few minutes later, a young woman squeezed into the elevator and demanded that I give her a chance to present her sales pitch. I told her we had already found the artist we wanted to represent. She would not listen and asked me to at least glance through her presentation once. Just then the power went off and we were stuck in the elevator.

Instead of panicking, the girl took out her mobile and, in the torchlight, began to show me her work. It was, without a doubt, superior to the one we had decided to represent. Another point that went completely in her favour was that she was the most beautiful woman I'd ever seen.

Within the few minutes that took the power to be restored, I had promised her a contract and finagled out a dinner date the same day to finalize the contract. She was smart, funny, and charming.

A few days later, after our first 'official' date, I knew she was 'The One'. After our second date, I knew we would get married and took her to meet my father. After our third date, we were essentially living together. If not for the power outage that day, perhaps I wouldn't have met my sweetheart, Rupa, who is notorious for being a latecomer everywhere. She promises to stay the same always. And I am happy to let her."

They all laughed. Rupa was smiling like a pampered child. She offered to be the next storyteller.

"Okay! Now that he has called me a latecomer, let me tell you how extraordinary my life has turned out to be ever since I met him. On the day I was to present the pitch, my taxi driver took me to a hotel at the other end of Bangalore which had the exact name as the one we were having the conference in. It turned out to be a spooky one used perhaps for clandestine purposes. I somehow escaped from there and found a taxi to the right hotel. Once I reached there, I came to know that another artist had won the contract.

I raced after this man and was trapped in the elevator. While on the way to meet him on our first official date, I got stuck in a traffic block for two straight hours, yet we enjoyed the two hours because he was caught in the same traffic block but a few kilometres away. We talked to each other nonstop for two hours and by the time we met for our date, we hit it off like old friends. When he took me to meet his father after our second date, I became aware that he planned to trap me forever.

And see what happened after we got engaged. We are in Chennai exactly when the worst flood in a century is wreaking havoc. Maybe something good will result from this too."

"I can guess what that might be," said Varun and made a gesture as if he was cradling a baby. Everyone burst into laughter.

Pratheesh raised his brows and wiggled them. Rupa narrowed her eyes.

"Who will go next?" asked Ramachandran who had taken on the role of the moderator.

Much to Tara's surprise, Mary volunteered to share her story next.

"I was moved by your stories. Stories of true love. In your story, Ramachandran, the death of your spouse felt like a curse to you. But for me, it came as a blessing. I hated the man I married. He was the devil incarnate himself. He abused me physically and emotionally every day. He was the worst sort of man you could imagine. He had very few friends and multiple enemies. You must be wondering why I tolerated the abuse. For me, I didn't have another choice.

I came from a poor family and my parents married me off to this rich bastard. They wouldn't support me in any way. So, one day, when he died in a car accident, I rejoiced. He left me a rich widow. I know I sound heartless. But for me, his death came as a blessing in disguise. Because his death had finally given me freedom. Freedom to raise my son in a loving environment. Freedom to fulfil his dreams. Freedom to show that love was all that mattered. Hearing your stories, I wish for a life filled with love for my son. But the one time he fell in love, he was burned at the stake for it. I hope he gets a second chance. He deserves it."

Tara bit her inner cheeks and tried to control her inner turmoil. She wanted to say something but she couldn't. How could she when her emotions were choking her? She looked down at her feet and remained silent.

"No, Mary. You have every right to think of his death as a blessing. Marriage is beautiful when it is built on the foundation of mutual love and respect. In many traditional marriages, that is far from reality. Many lives get sacrificed at the altar of marriage. So, Susheela are you ready to come up with your story."

"Yes. Many of you who know me think that I am a widow. But I am not sure if I am one. My husband was spiritually inclined from a young age and left home to find his spiritual guru when Varun was four. He left one Friday suddenly without any warning, leaving me and my kid alone in a strange city with no one to look after us. Initially, I was terrified. But soon, I understood that I couldn't wait for him to come and save us. I found a job at Varun's nursery as a teacher. I saved every paisa I could and taught myself via correspondence and short-term courses and finally retired as the principal of a prestigious local high school. I believe that by leaving us, my husband taught me the lesson that the only person I could rely on was myself. I don't have expectations from anyone. So, if someone does a good deed for me, it comes as a pleasant surprise. I am more in touch with myself because of the loss I suffered."

"You are quite a strong woman, Susheela. I am in awe of you," said Ramachandran.

Varun who was sitting next to Susheela pulled her closer and gave her a tight hug. Then clearing his throat, he spoke.

"I want to tell my story of hope next. You all have heard how my father left to seek his spiritual nirvana when I was four. Every day during my childhood, I nurtured the hope that he would return one day with bags full of gifts. I got bullied at school because I was the only one whose father was missing.

I was called a bastard, a vagabond and many other names. My only aim in life was to grow up fast enough and go in search of him. I would find him and bring him home and we would have a happy life together. When I was eighteen, I took a year off to travel. My mother didn't question me. She might have thought I wanted to go the same way as my father. But by then, I had begun to hate him for leaving us alone and escaping the hard life. I went with a group of wanderlust friends who were planning a trip to the Himalayas.

Every seeker of spirituality in India heads to the Himalayas to seek enlightenment. I went with them to Hrishikesh where I wandered amid groups of monks to gipsies. Seeking a long-forgotten face that might suddenly appear among them. Even after searching for six long months, I couldn't find him. But instead, the serene Himalayas beckoned to me and healed me from within.

Standing atop Mount Everest, I decided I wanted to see the world. I wanted to see more of this world and its magnificence. I had travelled to the summit of the world from the lap of the oceans. It felt like the correct path I had to take.

So, it was in a way my father who made me a traveller. Or rather travel is embedded in my genes. He travelled for enlightenment but I travel to seek the goodness in people. I have found kindness even in the worst places in the world. Inside a drug cartel in Mexico, within a gang of bandits in the deserts of Sahara, inside the red streets of Malaysia, I have found kindness everywhere. This flood itself is becoming an example where strangers are becoming the epitomes of love and kindness."

Applause greeted Varun's story. Tara knew that she could quit without speaking. But this was also her chance to tell Mary that she loved Manu and would love him always. And if she could muster the courage, she could even confess her truth. So, she began.

"When I landed in Chennai three days ago, I had no idea what lay in store for me. I was here to attend the launch of my debut novel. And now I am stranded here without having any contact with the world that I came from. I don't have any story of hope. I don't even know if I have any hope left for me in this world. But, I do have a story of love.

I fell in love with the father of my child while I was in college. We were immune to doubts and predictions of doom about our relationship. We weaved the dream of a happily ever after. We didn't care for the world and the only thing that mattered was love.

Yet, the world intruded and threw us apart. I was blinded by the veils of deceit and distrusted my one true love. When I realised my error, the father of my child was already lost to me. The man who once loved me has turned into a total stranger now. He doesn't trust me anymore. I wish I could tell him how much I love him."

Tara stopped because she couldn't talk anymore. She didn't dare to lift her head. She had targetted the story at Mary. For the others, it might have sounded like a common love story and that she was going through a bad time. Only Rupa and Mary could have understood what she meant.

It had been an impulsive decision to use the story sharing session to convey her message. Mary had not talked to her after that outburst a few days ago. But Tara didn't want to leave this house without telling her the truth. Though this would complicate things further, she felt a lot lighter.

"I am sure you will find a middle ground to solve your issues. It is human to err. Who is there in this room who hasn't committed a grave error in judgment? What is important is that we should try to correct our errors. And most situations are complicated by ego games. Leave your egos and tell him. That alone will help you find peace. Nothing else," said Susheela aunty.

Tara raised her head and gazed at Mary. Mary was staring at her. Her face was blank as though she was in shock.

Had she understood what she wanted to convey? She appeared pale. Dread began to creep through Tara. Had she overwhelmed Mary with the truth? She was still convalescing from the fever. Mary snapped out of the trance-like state she was in and walked out of the room without a word to anyone. Susheela went up to Varun and began talking to him earnestly.

"Okay people. I think we should all go to sleep. Varun did any message come from Manu?" asked Ramachandran.

"No. Nothing till now. The signals are terribly busy. It will be an uphill task to get connected."

"Yeah. True. Let us get some rest then. Things will be better by tomorrow."

One by one everyone began leaving the living room.

Rupa came to Tara and grabbed her hands. "Why did you do this? I won't lie, I have secretly hoped Manu was Aryan's father. Your declaration came as a shock to even me. Imagine how it must have been for Mary."

"I can't leave Chennai without letting Mary know that Aryan is her grandchild. She has the right to know. I won't be able to give her anything else."

"I don't think this will end well. She seemed to be in shock."

"I know. But I followed my gut instinct."

"Fingers crossed for you, my friend. I hope everything goes well for you." Rupa hugged Tara tightly.

18

Mary sat on the bed and watched Aryan sleeping peacefully. How had she missed the signs? Aryan looked exactly how Manu had been at this age. Also, he had similar likes and dislikes. She patted Aryan's cheeks and a sob escaped her.

The soft cheeks and the angelic face made her heart grow tender. She was his grandmother. When Aryan had first addressed her that way, it had felt so right. Now she knew why. He was indeed her grandchild. Her Manu's son! But the hatred towards his mother had stopped her from getting closer to the kid.

What should she do? Was Tara really saying the truth? Or was it some new game that she was playing?

She wouldn't allow her to tear apart Manu's life again. She needed answers and she better have them. She was not going to part with her grandson after being kept apart from him for so long.

Though Tara had told her story in front of everyone, she had cleverly disguised her story. No one except the ones who knew her would have understood who she was talking about. Her sole intention behind telling the story seemed to have been to let her know that Aryan was her grandchild. That much had become crystal clear to her. Would she have told the story if Manu had been present amidst them? She doubted that.

Aryan turned in his sleep and began mumbling something about Octonauts. Mary chuckled. Like father like son. Manu was also very vocal while dreaming. Mary recalled she had come to know about Tara via one such mumbling.

Mary heard someone gasp and looked up. Tara stood by the door. Oh, was she upset that she had come to see Aryan? Anger bubbled through her. Composing herself, Mary glared at Tara.

"Are you going to tell Manu about Aryan?"

"Yes. I will tell him before I leave Chennai."

"What do you think will happen when he knows the truth?"

"I don't know."

"I know. He will not allow you to keep his son away from him. Can you handle that?"

Tara didn't answer. How tangled could things get? When the truth was revealed to her, Mary didn't know how to tackle it. How had Tara held on to this secret for so long? Who else knew? Was her family privy to it? What about her husband?

"Does your husband know that he is raising the child of another man?"

"Yes. He knows. But he loves Aryan like his own."

"That is convenient. I feel pity for my son. You kept his son away from him for five years. I am not sure if love has made him immune to the anger he ought to feel towards you."

Tara didn't say anything. She seemed lost for words. Mary bent down and kissed Aryan's cheek and raked his hair with her fingers.

"I have only one request. You shattered my son's heart once. You are about to do it again. You are bound by marriage to another man. Don't give him false hopes. Don't tell him about Aryan if you can't allow him to be his father. I beg you."

"Keeping him in the dark was never my intention. Whatever happened was beyond my control. I have no idea how he is going to react or what the outcome would be. Manu deserves to know the truth. "

The words sounded genuine and Mary's heart filled with pity for Tara.

"I used to think of you as my own daughter. Tell me what led to all this. I want to know everything. I know my son's side of the story. I need to hear yours."

For the next half an hour, Mary listened as Tara talked about the deceit her sister had played out. Through her words, Mary felt the pain she had undergone. Who would believe now that blood was thicker than water? Mary's heart went out to the girl who sat near her with eyes glazed with unshed tears. Tara told her she had searched for Manu everywhere without success.

"I tried to forget him and move on. But I have not been a wife in the true sense to my husband. I am living a lie. I cannot be Manu's and I will never truly belong to Karthik. That is my punishment for distrusting Manu."

Mary sighed and held Tara's hands in hers.

"We will find a way. Maybe Karthik would want you to return to Manu now that you have found him. He was very understanding till now, right?"

"Yes, he has been. But we had a huge row before I left home this time. He called me while we were at the airport. He wants me to return to Bangalore as his wife. I think he wants a real relationship from now on. What worries me now is that he is not answering my calls. Nor has he called me. He is never like this."

Mary was taken aback. How could a man and woman live under the same roof and maintain the kind of platonic relationship that Karthik had with Tara? If not love, what had prompted Karthik to support Tara?

Or was it because he loved her truly that he didn't try to force himself on her? Though his latest action seemed confusing. In a situation such as this, even enemies would call to enquire about one's wellbeing.

"Is everything alright with him? I think you should check with his friends or family. This is definitely not something a normal man would do. "

"I called and told my family about my whereabouts. If something was wrong, they would have known. My sister is travelling. She called me yesterday from Dubai. Today she will reach Bangalore. She said she will enquire and call me. I am waiting for her call."

"Does she know you are here? I mean in Manu's house?"

"No. I didn't tell her. She will raise a ruckus if she knew."

"Good. Better keep it that way. We will find a way out of all this. And I hope I get you and my grandchild back. You deserve a full life, Tara. Don't live a farce."

"I will find a way out of this. I need to."

Tara picked up her phone, which she had kept for charging using the power bank she had borrowed from Varun.

"Oh, God! Ranjini called me thrice while we were down in the living room. Let me call and see if she has any news about Karthik."

Mary waited as Tara called her sister. After the call went through, Mary watched as Tara's face went pale. She sat on the edge of the bed as she listened to what her sister was telling her. From the way she grabbed at the sheets and sat numbly on the bed, Mary guessed the news was bad. From the words Tara uttered in query or reply, she deduced that something was wrong with Karthik. She waited patiently for the call to end.

Once she disconnected the call, Tara covered her eyes with her palm and continued to remain silent.

"What happened, Tara? Is everything alright?"

After a long minute, Tara answered. "Karthik met with an accident the day we left for Chennai. That was the reason he wasn't answering my calls."

Mary gasped. "How is he now? Is it bad?"

"He is still in the ICU. He is stable but not conscious yet."

"Thank God. Who is with him now? Anyone other than your sister?"

"My in-laws have arrived there now. They didn't know anything about it until today morning when my sister called them."

This certainly changed things. Tara would want to return as soon as possible. From what she knew of the girl, she was not the one who shirked from responsibilities. Now her husband needed her more than Manu.

As though confirming this, Tara addressed her. "Aunty, I know I will have to return to Karthik. I will have to keep all this hidden from him for now. I don't think I can tell him about Manu now."

"I understand. You should do the right thing, Tara. As soon as things return to normal, go to Karthik. But promise me, you will tell everything to Manu soon."

"I stick by my earlier decision. I will tell Manu about Aryan. I won't lie to him. But I don't know if telling him now would be a prudent step."

"Yes, you are right. Don't tell him anything now. It will only complicate things further. Go home, talk with Karthik and then decide."

Mary walked out of Tara's room with a heavy heart. She didn't know how things would pan out. She selfishly hoped that in the end, her Manu would find happiness. That she would have a complete family to cherish.

19

Manu returned home at around three in the morning. He let himself in using his spare key with the intention of not disturbing anyone. He found that Varun was still up.

"Manu...Good to see you, pal. How is Dhananjay?"

"I have good news, man! Dhananjay is out of danger. The angioplasty was successful."

"Just what we needed to hear. Do they need anything? Any help?"

"No, nothing. I have other news as well. Soumya is pregnant. She fainted at the hospital and the doctors ran a few tests on her. She will return home once Dhananjay is released by the hospital. He is being kept under observation."

"Wow. That calls for a double celebration. Others will be so relieved. Especially our mothers. They were the ones who took it really bad."

"Are they all okay? The hospital is bursting with patients."

"They are perfectly fine. We found a unique way to cope with the situation. We shared stories. You should have heard them. I am writing them all down."

"I will change and come. Then I will hear them. Also, I have something to discuss with you. We might be able to do some emergency volunteer work if you are up to it."

"Sure. We will talk after you return."

Manu went to his room out of habit and it was only when he entered the room that he remembered Tara was sleeping in his room. He stood and watched her lying on his bed with Aryan and Rupa fondly. The vista filled his mind with peace. Tara turned in her sleep then and Manu held his breath. While she continued to sleep, he grabbed a tracksuit from the cupboard without making any noise and tiptoed out of the room.

When he returned to the study after a quick shower in the common area bathroom, Varun was writing in his journal.

"Okay. I am all ears. Tell me the stories."

Varun began to narrate the stories. The stories were indeed fascinating. When it was Tara's turn, Manu leaned forward, his head raised and fully alert. As the others had shared stories that disclosed secrets, he was sure Tara's story would be equally intriguing.

As Tara's story unfolded, a chill slowly enveloped him. Was this true? Had he misheard?

"Did you say she fell in love with the father of her child while in college?" Manu asked in a shaky, disbelieving voice.

"Yes. But the sad thing is that they went separate ways. Poor girl. Outwardly, she appears so calm and happy. Inside, she seems like a total mess."

Manu stood up and walked towards the window. He braced the window with both hands drawing in slow, steady breaths. At first, he couldn't believe what he had heard. Aryan was his son?

Then, as the moments he had spent together with Aryan flashed through his mind, he became convinced more and more that Aryan was his blood. Tara had kept such a huge secret from him? What else was she hiding? How could she do this to him? He needed answers. It couldn't wait.

Varun, who had been continuing his narration, stopped and stared as Manu kicked a chair out of his way and stormed out of the room.

When Manu entered his room this time, Tara was wide awake. Perhaps his hurried footsteps had woken her up. She sat up on the bed and mouthed his name.

Wordlessly, he went to her and grabbed her right arm. He led her out of the room and onto the roof shed on the terrace. Once there, he let go of her forcefully and scooted away to maintain a safe distance between them. He needed the distance to keep himself sane and in control.

The question had been quietly burning a hole in his heart ever since he had heard her story from Varun. Yet when he addressed it to Tara, his voice sounded like thunder rolling.

"Is Aryan my child?"

Tara cringed and stared at him with something akin to fear in her eyes.

Her silence confirmed his suspicions.

"How could you? All these years? Am I to be surprised by you at every turn? I did not deserve this. Clearly, I didn't deserve this."

The fear and helplessness that he saw in Tara's eyes were now gone. It seemed like the calm before a storm. As expected, the storm broke in the next minute.

"Of course, you didn't deserve it. But did I deserve to go through it? You were the one who walked away from me. You were the one who did not even reply to my emails. I tried in every possible way to find you. Don't even think that I tried to cheat you out of this, Manu. I would have wanted you near me but unluckily you weren't near. I went through everything alone. If you had stayed and fought, instead of just walking away, things might have been different."

"So, I am the coward now? Is that why I had to hear the truth about my own child from a stranger? If Varun had not told me the story you told everyone, would I even know that Aryan was my child?"

Tara looked away and then paced around in the shed silently as if she couldn't trust herself to speak. After a while, she turned and addressed Manu.

"Manu, please listen. Understand me. I beg you. I came to know I was pregnant with Aryan after you left. I had to marry Karthik quickly for the sake of our child. Karthik helped me by giving his name to our child. If not for him, my family would have forced me to abort the child. None of them knows that you are Aryan's father."

Manu scoffed, refusing to believe a word in Tara's confession. Karthik accepted his child without any objection and married her for keeping her secret safe? It seemed like a total cock and bull story. But Aryan's face flashed before his mind's eye and he wanted to believe in her story. He loved the child. Just yesterday he had wished he could call the child his own. In a bizarre turn of fate, his wish was now a reality.

"You told your story to everyone. Everyone except me. They don't even know that I am the man mentioned in the story. Your unfortunate lover, the father of your child. I guess the story was aimed at my mother. Did it work?"

"Yes. She knows. She understands me."

"Oh, does she? So, I am the idiot who doesn't understand."

"Manu, please. I'll explain everything."

"You will? Why now? We met three days ago. Three days. You had enough time to tell me if you really wanted to do so." Manu could think of multiple instances when they had been alone. She could have told him at the mall. She could have told him last night. If she was in earnest, she would have found a million ways to tell him.

"Manu, you are deliberately being difficult. Hear me out."

Manu turned away from her and scooted towards the bedroom door. He didn't want to hear any more excuses. He had never thought he could hate her. But he hated her now more than anything in the world. He hated the words that were tumbling out of her mouth. He hated her very presence.

"I don't want to hear anything. I want my child. I won't allow you to take him away from me again. You owe me five long years. I have missed the best moments of his growing up years. I don't want to miss another moment."

Tara lifted her right hand as if she wanted to stop him. He took another step away from her. He didn't want to be near her anymore.

Manu walked into the bedroom and sat on the bed next to Aryan. As though he was disturbed by the movement of the bed, Aryan turned around in his sleep and in doing so, he huddled closer to Manu. Manu's eyes misted. He patted him on his arms to lull him back to sleep.

He had loved Aryan from the moment he had met him. But now, he was meeting his son, touching him as his father. Excitement, joy and contentment raced through his heart. He resisted the urge to lift the little man and swing him around. His son, his blood. His pulse raced and he felt a lightness in his chest as his lips curved into a smile.

Was this how every new parent felt? Did Tara experience this when she first saw Aryan? Did she also feel this incredible need to make him feel safe beyond any ripple of a doubt?

Manu caressed his soft cheeks, raked his fingers through his silky hair and leaned down to place a gentle kiss on his cheeks. He swallowed a lump in his throat as emotions began to choke him. His boy was five years old. He had missed so much. He hadn't sung lullabies to make him sleep. He hadn't changed his diapers. He hadn't cheered him on as he took his first steps. He hadn't seen him cry on the first day of school. He hadn't taught him the alphabet or numbers. Losses. He would never get to experience them.

The memory from the other night when he had fallen asleep near Aryan now returned as a tender wound. How much had he wished then for Aryan to be his child? She could have told him then. They had even shared a kiss. Like old times. Yet she hadn't told him. Tara's betrayal stung. She had been with him for three days. She could have told him any time. His anger began bubbling up again.

A single glance at Aryan and his anger dissipated. Manu picked up his slender arms and placed tiny kisses all over his palms. Aryan giggled in sleep as Manu continued raining kisses on him. Manu's face lit up with a smile. Maybe his overnight stubble had tickled him. Manu got up after pressing another kiss on his forehead.

Tara stood at the door watching him. He glowered at her. He heard her feebly whispering his name as he stomped past her. He had to find a way to keep his boy with him. He won't allow his child to be raised by a stranger.

Even if that meant separating Aryan from his own mother.

20

"Did you hear about the Bhatts? I am thrilled. I heard it from Varun," asked Susheela aunty.

Tara nodded her head. It had been Varun who had told her as well.

Susheela aunty had cheered up at the news and was now single-handedly making *rava dosas* for the entire gang. Tara and Rupa had been given the charge of making the sambar to go with it. Because they had very few vegetables that were in good condition except a few potatoes and tomatoes, the sambar lacked its richness. But the way everyone devoured it, made them feel they had made the tastiest curry in the whole world. Hunger was the best appetiser. Susheela aunty had generously supplied her stash of homemade chutney powder, much to the happiness of all in the team.

The men appeared to be in great spirits, except for Manu whose face shouted that he hadn't slept a single wink the whole night. Grimacing, Tara bit her lips. This was entirely her fault.

Manu had made Aryan sit near him and had taken over the charge of feeding him the *dosas*. He was bribing him with stories and Aryan had already eaten more than his usual quota.

"Aryan, you can stop eating if you've had enough," Tara said, just to get their attention.

Both father and son ignored her and continued bonding over breakfast. After a while, Aryan began feeding dosa pieces to Manu who seemed to completely enjoy the experience. Soon, Aryan had smeared the sambar-dosa mixture all over Manu's face. Aryan was asking for tissues to clean up the mess. Of course, he had to show off his expertise in handling such culinary disasters.

When Tara handed over the tissues to Aryan, Manu smiled fondly at him as he wiped tidbits of dosa from his chin and lips. Tara's lips curved watching them. Manu's face clouded when he saw her smile.

"So, champ, we are done, right? Can I get up now? You need to wash your hands and mouth as well," Manu said to Aryan and the duo left the table together.

Rupa who had been sitting next to Tara and observing their interaction turned to her.

"Yup. He knows. Varun told him. He hates me now," Tara said, answering the question Rupa was burning to ask.

Rupa stiffened and stared at her incredulously. Tara should have listened to her and told Manu when she had the chance. But she wondered if that would have made a difference. She had expected this. No matter when she told him, this would have been his reaction. He had the right to be furious.

"Did you tell him about Karthik?"

"No. He didn't give me a chance to speak."

"Relax. We will find a way to make him understand."

Taking another dosa from the casserole, Rupa passed it to Tara taking in her empty plate. Tara accepted it without much thought. After dipping pieces of it into the sambar, she began stuffing it into her mouth. Stress was making her heart pound and her belly ache. Binge eating had been her way of dealing with stress. Knowing her, Rupa continued to pass dosas to her and Tara indulged herself by numbing herself with food.

Susheela aunty and Mary joined them then and Susheela began to talk about how the water level was beginning to recede.

"Though I would love to forget everything that happened in the last few days like a bad dream, I realize now that not all things have been bad. If not for the flood, I would not have met you all."

"Yes. Things are never totally black or white. Most of the time they are grey, a mixture of black and white. It really depends on what we give attention to," said Rupa.

Tara's gaze flitted to Mary who looked up just then. Were Mary's eyes accusing her of the stressful situation she had put Manu into? She was not sure.

Manu had hardly eaten. If not for Aryan, he would have left the table without eating anything.

While Tara was washing the dishes, Mary came in to help.

"Do not back away, Tara. Talk to him. He will listen," she said softly, but her face didn't reflect the same confidence. Mary had been silently observing Manu ever since he came down to breakfast and seemed to have deduced what might have happened.

"I will," Tara said. Wiping the last one of the dishes, she arranged them back in the overhead drawer and turned to Mary. "I will try to make him understand, aunty. But if he doesn't, I don't know how to deal with it. I can't stand his hatred. I am crumbling inside."

"Everything is going to be fine. I know my son. This anger is temporary. Don't give up on him. I have seen him grieve when he lost you. He still loves you, Tara. Talk to him. Make him listen."

Aryan's laughter from the living room drew their attention and they moved in to check. They were playing 'the giant and his food' game. Manu, the giant, was super hungry. He had rolled up Aryan in a blanket like a big tortilla and was pretending to be eating him. With each pretend-bite on the blanket, Aryan laughed out loud. After taking a few 'bites', the giant placed the tortilla on the couch exclaiming he was full. Within seconds, the tortilla demanded to be eaten again. The giant complied.

Tara's heart grew warm watching them. When she turned to Mary, she saw her biting her lower lip in a bid to control her tears. Tara wanted to hug her close and apologise for depriving her of many such moments that she would have cherished. She had always loved Mary. And that made her guilt weigh her down even more.

Mary nudged her then and whispered," I will find a way to take Aryan with me. You talk to him. Okay?" Walking towards the duo, Mary joined the game and Aryan's giggles filled the room once more.

After a few minutes, Mary walked away from the living room with Aryan perched on her hips. Tara didn't know what enticement she had used, but Aryan had forgotten his giant already.

The moment Manu realised that Tara was the only other person left in the living room, he got up to leave. He walked into the now empty study and sat at his table and switched on his laptop.

He glared at Tara when she followed him into the room and snapped, "I have some work to do. Leave me alone."

Tara stood at the door watching him turn his attention to the laptop, his face crimson with anger. Had his love turned to a fog of hatred? Tara decided to dive straight into it, needing him to listen to her. She would explain everything to him, appeal to the love that he once had for her. Beseech for kindness to the man who still owned her heart.

With that decision made, she stepped into the room and forced herself to walk toward him with legs that suddenly seemed like they were made of jelly.

"Manu, we need to talk." Tara's hands shook and she clasped them together. "You have to listen to me."

Silence filled the room as Manu glowered at her. His thick eyebrows shot up.

"What if I don't want to hear anything?" Manu asked, staring straight at her.

Tara swallowed and looked away. She shook her head to remind herself that the man before him wasn't the same youth who had been head over heels in love with her. She had no power over Manu now. It might prove disastrous to try and talk to him, yet, she was determined to try. Her deepest desire then was to be heard by him.

She won't quit trying. She stood firmly and fixed her gaze on Manu.

21

Tara represented all his failures. Even now when his anger was making it difficult for him to breathe, he couldn't bear to see the tears that glistened in her eyes. Manu closed his laptop and leaned back in his chair, locking his gaze with Tara's.

If he had to get back his composure, he needed to get everything out of his system. Every single question that had troubled him till now needed an answer. Tara had to answer him. He did not plan to make it easy for her.

"Why should I listen to you? You haven't given me any reason to trust you. You have told nothing but lies ever since we met."

"What lies?"

"You made me believe you were leading a happily married life right from the moment we met at the bookstore. It didn't make me long to understand that you were trying too hard to convince me. But I couldn't understand why you would go to such lengths to hurt me. To make me feel like a sad loser."

Tara's eyes blazed with anger.

"I did nothing of the sort. You are imagining things."

"Oh really? So, those carefully crafted sentences weren't aimed to make me jealous, were they? You were just talking about your happy married life."

"You think I led a happy life? It was hell. How could I when all I could think about was you?"

Manu's heart skipped a beat. He wanted to believe her. But, how could he? All the facts proved the opposite.

"You won't get anywhere with your lies. If you were in love with me, you would have told me everything at the first opportunity you got."

"You think I didn't try? In your eyes, I went ahead and married Karthik to secure a happy future for myself. You forgot that I sent mail after mail to try and contact you. You didn't reply to even one mail. You deleted your social media accounts. I agree I made a mistake. But you didn't give me a chance to correct it. Will you please listen to me at least now?"

The pain in her voice crowded the room. Was he repeating the same error he had committed all those years ago? Had that cost him his son? He had refused to listen to her then. He had quit using his old Yahoo email account and created a new one on Gmail after reaching Chennai. He had wanted a fresh start.

He will hear her out. Closing his eyes, he took a deep breath. He then directed her to sit in front of him. He could at least make this civil.

Tara remained silent and seemed like she was afraid that the first word she uttered would disturb the peace that currently prevailed in the room. He drummed on the table to urge her to talk like he used to when they were in college. Though it had been subconsciously done, it did the trick. Tara began to talk.

"From the very beginning, I wanted to tell you everything. At the mall, I tried but you were not ready to listen. Then the other night I came down to talk to you after you left. But aunty's fever kept us occupied. When I shared that story with the others, I had decided to tell you everything myself when you returned from the hospital. I merely took that opportunity, to tell the truth to your mother. She would not have listened to me otherwise. That was my best chance to tell her the truth because nobody except your mother and Rupa would have understood my secret." Tara paused.

"What now? Do you plan to keep me away from my son? Trust me, I won't allow you."

"Manu, don't say that. I can't do that to Karthik now."

"Watch me. If you are done with your confessions, please leave."

Tara swallowed and cleared her throat as if she was finding it difficult to speak. Was she about to say that she had fallen in love with Karthik? That Aryan loved him and she didn't want to separate them. Despair and anger invaded his heart.

"I haven't told you everything. Karthik met with an accident three days ago, the same afternoon that we left for Chennai. He had not been answering my calls all these days as he was in the ICU. I came to know of this only yesterday night after I shared the story with the others. Your mother agreed with me then that perhaps it was not the right time to share the story with you."

Manu didn't know what to say. Why were things always so complicated when it came to them? How could he blame her now? And wasn't Karthik the reason his son was alive and well? His anger slowly melted away as the minutes ticked by and concern filled his thoughts.

"How is he now?"

"I don't have any more updates. I will have to return as early as possible."

"Yes. I understand. It might still take a few more days for things to return to normal here. I will try and book you on the first available flight. I will come with you."

"Thank you. I want you to know that if I had any way of changing what happened to us, I would have changed it. I love you, Manu."

Manu had difficulty responding.

"I wish I could hope we could be together. I want it so badly but I can't do this to Karthik. Especially not now. He needs me."

"But Tara, I have lost five years with my son. How can I live away from him after today? I have missed so much already."

Hearing his words, Tara began to tap on her phone until she found what she was looking for. She handed the phone to Manu when she found what she had been looking for. She had accessed her website using the phone browser.

"I know this is perhaps too little and too late. But this was the only way I could think of preserving memories for you. I have uploaded photos and videos in this particular section on my website which is password protected. Only the person with the password can see the contents. Your name is the password. If you go through those, perhaps you might find a way to be a part of Aryan's growing years. I wrote on the page on every significant occasion in the last five years. Read through it when you get time."

Tara stood up and quickly walked away after retrieving the phone from his hands.

He would have to make the maximum out of the time he now had with Aryan in the coming hours. Could there be a way to get him and Tara to stay in his life forever? He had no idea how that could happen.

If the floods had taught him anything, it was that he had to live in the moment. The next moment would take care of itself if the present moment was lived well. Hindsight often brought in regret. He had to find a way to make the hours with them count.

Before that, he wanted to go through the archives of the section of Tara's blog and retrieve as many memories as he could. To view milestones from the life of his child.

Firing his laptop, Manu connected to the Wi-Fi Varun had set up in the house and entered the section of Tara's website she had asked him to check.

The section was aptly named 'Memorabilia' and Manu accessed it after typing the password. There were innumerable entries and each one was tagged with the time and had photos or videos embedded. The one thing the entries had in common was that every single entry was addressed to him.

22

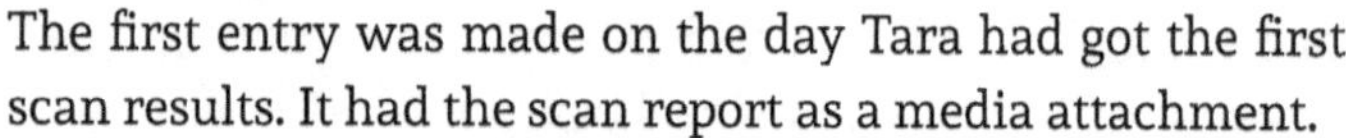

The first entry was made on the day Tara had got the first scan results. It had the scan report as a media attachment.

Dearest Manu,

I have mailed you so many times. Your phone number is not in use. Tell me, how I can contact you? When are you going to return? Won't you ever forgive me?

I saw our baby. He/ she is so tiny. I wished we could together hear our baby's heartbeat for the first time. But alas, it wasn't to be. I have decided to record memories online so that when we finally meet, you are not going to complain that I am a bad memory keeper. I will update this page whenever possible.

I am excited but I am scared as hell as well. I hope our baby will be strong and healthy and make it to the delivery day. I don't care that I am sick every single day and feel exhausted. I don't care if our baby is a boy or a girl. All I wish for now is that you would be near me when our baby enters this world.

I am already so much in love with our baby.

The next blog post was after she had felt the baby kick for the first time during the second trimester. It was accompanied by the picture of Tara with her baby bump already showing. She had her palms spread on her stomach as if she was caressing her baby.

Dearest Manu,

Our son kicked me today. He (I am pretty sure it is a he though the doctor refuses to tell me) is pretty naughty. Always keeps rolling around. Can you believe that within a few months, we will be able to hold him?

I don't have morning sickness anymore and my mother keeps insisting that I eat for two. If you see me now, you won't even recognise me. I have put on five kilos already. At this rate, I am going to become quite fat by the time I become a mother.

I have been thinking all day as to what I would name him. We had never discussed such things. We were busy talking about silly things. We didn't even ever picture ourselves as parents. Anyway, I have decided to name our baby Aryan if he is a boy and Arya in case we have a girl.

Where are you, Manu? I search your name online daily and all the faces that stare back at me are those of strangers.

Please, are you listening? Return to me, Manu.

When he reached the last line, Manu's heart became overwhelmed with emotions. He quickly clicked on the next post.

"It is a boy," screamed the headline. It had been written on the 7th day after Aryan's birth. A cute picture of Aryan all wrapped up, with only his tiny face visible, accompanied the post.

Dearest Manu,

Meet Aryan. He is the cutest little thing you would ever see. Don't go by his cute looks though. Can you believe that he kept the four of us, including the home nurse we hired, on our toes the whole night? He screamed his lungs out for being pushed out of the cosy little confine of my tummy that had been his home for nine months.

Firstly, he surprised us by coming seven days earlier than the delivery date. He took his time to arrive and kept me in labour for twelve scary hours. Yet, when I finally heard his shrill cries and held him for the first time, all I could do was cry happy tears. Who would have thought that a pink, soft, cuddly baby could evoke so many emotions all at once? And I missed you terribly.

How will I ever give these moments to you, Manu?

Aryan reminds me of you every moment. The only thing that calms him down is music. If I hum a lullaby he immediately stops crying. He takes after you. Can you guess what his favourite lullaby is?

As the hours passed, Manu devoured the snippets from the life of his son one after the other. He knew the exact date he had turned on his tummy, the date he had his first solid food, the day he started crawling. Every post had more photos now and shorter descriptions.

Manu laughed when he watched a video of Aryan crawling around with curd smeared on his entire body refusing to be cleaned up. Apparently, he had overturned the curd bowl and then played with the spilt curd. He felt the pain when his baby cried after being vaccinated.

The post she had written on Aryan's first birthday was the longest to date. It had lots of photos also. Photos of Tara with Aryan made his heart grow warm.

Dearest Manu,

Our son turned one today. 365 days have passed since your son arrived in my life. And I have not heard from you or about you till now.

Have you forgotten me completely? Not a day passes without me remembering you. I wake up crying at night and hope you were near. Our baby reminds me of you every minute. Though I carried him in my womb for nine months, he has taken entirely after you. He likes the colour green just like you. Guess what his favourite vegetable is? Yes, carrot. Same as yours. He loves payasam and eats it till his tummy becomes round like a ball. I do know someone else who behaves the same way.

He can spend hours on his piano lost in the world of music. He has already learned his ABCs and 123s. Quite smart like his father. I have to read a story to him every night and he goes to sleep only after hearing a couple of lullabies. Do you remember how you used to make me sing to you every night? Your son is continuing the tradition.

I know you will never find this post or read this unless I give you the password. But it doesn't matter. I look forward to recording these moments of joy for you. Even if I never meet you, I will continue doing this. While I type these notes, I feel you are near. I am able to fool myself into thinking that one day you will read these notes and thank me for creating these memorabilia.

It is quite possible that the next time we meet, you will have someone holding onto your arm and you will introduce her to me as your wife. Maybe you will have become a father yourself by then. Or maybe you will ignore me completely and walk on. I don't know what destiny has written in my stars, but I will continue to write these notes to you in this secret online journal.

I hope one day you would read this. And if you do read this, then I want you to know that I still love you and always will.

Every turn on the road gives me hope that I might meet you the next moment. It doesn't matter that it always ends in despair.

Do return to us, Manu. I miss you. We miss you.

A veil of tears blurred his vision and he looked away from the screen. Both of them, Tara and he had erred.

Humans err. We always did stuff that we regretted. Given a chance, we would trade anything in the world to undo our mistakes. Yet such moments repeat, where we become powerless. We realized then that perhaps there is a higher power at work that is far stronger than us, our stubborn needs and goals.

Manu leaned back on his chair and raised his head to the heavens and sent a heartfelt prayer. *Oh Lord in heaven, don't take away the love of my life yet again.*

Every post he had read had made him realise the extent to which Tara loved him. Every sweet memory embedded in those posts had pumped energy into him. And with every word, he had determined that he should find a way to keep the two people he loved most in the world close to him. He was even willing to talk to Karthik.

If he had to go the legal way, he would. There was no way he would be satisfied with these virtual memories alone. He wanted to create new memories of his own with them. Memories that would assault his senses with their smell, sound and feel. He would have it no other way.

23

Except for Manu, who according to Varun, was busy with his laptop in the study and lost to the world, all the others had gathered around the dining table for some fresh coffee and biscuits. Hope flooded Tara's heart.

Was he going through her blog posts? Would they make him angrier or would they bring the old loving Manu back to them? She didn't know. She could only wish that all would turn out well.

Varun and Pratheesh had gone down to inspect the ground floor which was now free from flood water. Though the flood water had receded, the floor was knee-deep with dirt. Susheela aunty, who had accompanied him, was sitting silently.

"We will help clean up the mess. Don't worry. I think we should leave it for now. We should wait for confirmation from the authorities," said Ramachandran. All the others agreed.

"Also, we have to take precautions. It will be the breeding ground for so many disease-causing bacteria. We will have to wait till we can gather the supplies. Else we will be inviting diseases," said Varun.

After much thought, Tara took a glass of coffee and headed to the study accompanied by a chattering Aryan and Varun. Manu was leaning back on his chair and appeared to have fallen asleep.

Upon Varun's insistence, Aryan climbed onto his lap and pressed a kiss on Manu's cheeks. Manu opened his eyes and on seeing Aryan, gathered him close and kissed the top of his head. He then looked up and his eyes met hers. They were devoid of the anger she had found in them a few hours before. Instead, a twinkle glittered in his eyes reminding her of the lover she still dreamed about.

Hope raised its audacious head once again within the depths of her heart.

Manu protested as Aryan slipped out from his arms and raced out of the room following Varun who had headed out of the room with his camera.

Tara handed the coffee to Manu. Their gaze locked and lingered as he took the coffee from her. There was hope for them, wasn't there? Breaking the moment, her phone began to ring. It was Ranjini. Did she have more news?

Excusing herself, she walked to the balcony to attend the call.

"How is Karthik now? Were you able to talk to him?

"He is conscious now. I met him a few minutes ago."

"Thank God. I will be there as soon as I can."

"He is conscious but the prognosis is not good. Brace yourself. I am sorry to be the bearer of bad news. The accident injured his spine badly. According to the tests, he will remain a paraplegic for life."

Tara forgot to breathe for the next several seconds. Paraplegic? She knew what that word meant. It meant Karthik would lose the use and feeling below the waist, affecting his legs, hips and other body functions. Paraplegics never recovered. Was Karthik doomed to spend the rest of his life in a wheelchair?

"Tara, you there? I am so sorry."

"Does he know about it yet? I can't even imagine the pain he would have gone through."

"He doesn't know the full extent of his injuries yet. The doctors haven't told him yet. The accident was terrible. I was at the accident site yesterday."

Ranjini disconnected the call a while later after urging Tara to remain strong. Tara didn't know what to do. Her heart went out to the man who had never done anything other than good towards her. She regretted that she would never see him run around chasing little Aryan in their house. Karthik was a man who never depended on others. He wore his independence like a badge. How would he cope?

When Tara walked back into the room, Manu's eyes met hers. He seemed to sense her unease.

Tara quickly told him about Karthik. He held her hands and squeezed them. Tara struggled to suppress her sobs. Manu gathered her in a calming hug. Tara sobbed and allowed herself to relax on his chest.

"I am sorry to hear that, Tara. But, relax. All will be well. I will accompany you to Bangalore. He needs you now. Poor Aryan. He will become upset if he sees Karthik that way."

"I wish I could leave now. Maybe via road or train."

"We will check. But the fastest and safest way will be via plane. With the floods receding, air travel will resume soon. Things will get back to normal in the next twenty-four hours according to experts. Let's hope they are correct."

While they talked, Tara prayed that the experts who had pronounced that Karthik would be a paraplegic for life were wrong. Nothing justified his ordeal.

This accident also meant that life the way she knew was going to end. Things would have to change. Her habits, her way of life and her lifestyle. Karthik had been the bread-earner in their family and she had been content being a stay-at-home mom pursuing her passion for writing. She would have to find a job to support themselves. With Karthik ending up in a wheelchair, it will be like having another kid to manage.

Tara was sure of one thing. Karthik would face this bravely. He would adapt to this new way of life without any complaint. The man lived by plans. And he would create elaborate plans to find ways to adapt himself to the new situation. She wouldn't be surprised if he proved the doctors wrong and walked again. He was stubborn when it came to his dreams and ambitions. He won't give up easily.

She poured out all her worries to Manu. He listened patiently. Before long, she didn't feel suffocated by the thoughts that were running around in loops in her mind.

"Count on me for any sort of help. I have a friend with a paraplegic sister who leads a near to normal life. She works in an MNC. I'll ask him for help."

"Yes. We will need lots of guidance."

Just then Tara heard Aryan calling her and turned to go when Manu stopped her by holding on to her hand.

"Before you go, I want you to understand this. Don't be tensed by what I told you in the morning. I want you to go to Karthik and be with him without any doubts or second thoughts. All I want is for you and Aryan to be happy."

Manu's words reminded her of why she had fallen in love with him in the first place. She had fallen in love with the youth whose kindness had touched her heart most. Tara momentarily closed her eyes and let the warmth of his words spread through her. Opening her eyes, she stared into his. This decision must not have been easy for him. Yet, she could trust him to always take the right decision. He would never play with anyone's life.

"And remember, I love you. And I always will. Nothing will ever change that," he said, the pain in his voice clear. Tara walked back into the study while her heart reeled in misery. Her heart needed more time to understand what was crystal clear to her mind already. Their paths were about to diverge yet another time.

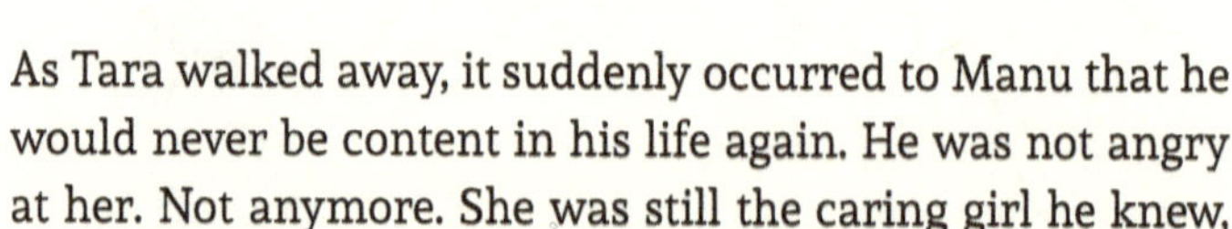

As Tara walked away, it suddenly occurred to Manu that he would never be content in his life again. He was not angry at her. Not anymore. She was still the caring girl he knew, who always put others before herself. Selfless and loving.

But his future was being moulded by infinite sadness. How could he be happy when the girl he had ever loved was going away once again? This time, the split seemed to be final.

He walked into the balcony to calm himself down. The vista before his eyes was definitely not one that could calm a disturbed heart. Yet somehow, it showed him the bigger picture. Everywhere his eyes went, he saw only gloom. Dreams were being washed away. Silent cries for help from strangers. His sorrow was insignificant compared to the losses of many others caught in the flood. He had, in fact, gained a son.

Someone touched his right shoulder before leaning on the balcony right next to him. It was Varun.

"I owe you an apology. I had no idea that you were the hero of Tara's story. I understand that it was not my story to tell. I hope I didn't make things worse for you two. Tara appeared to be almost on the verge of tears."

"No apology expected. You didn't know. Also, if not for you, I might have never known. We are never meant to be together. That is what I have understood."

"Sorry but I don't agree. Just now when I had come in to take my notebook from your desk, your laptop screen refreshed and I saw the blog post you were reading. I am sorry but I read what she had written to you. I am convinced that she loves you more than anyone else. I don't want you to give up on her. Trust me, she will return to you. And Aryan is a sweetheart. How can you stay away from him now that you know?"

"They might have come to me. I would have put up a fight. But now is not the time."

"Why do you say so?"

"Destiny has again thrown a rogue card at us. Her husband met with an accident. Worse, he is now a paraplegic. I know Tara. She will never leave him now. She will dedicate the rest of her life to making his life better."

"Paraplegic? But why did she marry him in the first place when she loved you?"

"It is a long story."

"I would love to hear."

"I will tell you all the gory details of our tragic love story. But we have work to do."

Varun grimaced. Manu insisted that his story could wait. He needed to distract himself from the dilemma that he faced. Though he had promised Tara all help, he didn't know how he would deal with another parting.

Manu turned to Varun and explained what Raghu, the friend he had made at the hospital had asked him to do. As expected, Varun was eager to help.

"Yes. Of course. I am already using my Twitter and FB accounts to spread awareness and share SOS messages from people who need help. The number of tweets out there is mind-numbing. As you said, if we can set up a small coordination cell right here, it can be of great use to the community. I am sure Pratheesh and Ramachandran would also help. Since power hasn't been restored yet, I think I will have to take out the secret weapon that I have been saving for emergencies. Come with me, let me show it to you."

Varun led Manu towards a big box they had retrieved from his house. Opening it, Varun proudly displayed a lithium-powered power generator.

"Splendid! This is amazing!" Manu exclaimed, recognising the environment-friendly power generator, which was often featured in their science magazine because of its many advantages.

"Meet the badass who has seen me through many power outages and travels. Zero fumes, zero noise and an easy-to-use, plug-and-play way to power all my essential electronics and appliances at the push of a button. It's safe enough to store inside any home or apartment for running lights or appliances during an emergency power outage. Yet it is durable enough to take along to your next outdoor project. My pet device can be recharged with solar energy or through the wall and the AC outlet. It cost a bomb but was worth every penny I spent. Helped me out many times already."

"Okay. Let us put your secret weapon to use, then. Set it up. I will call Raghu and ask him to email me the procedure for setting up our control station. Will ask Pratheesh and Ramachandran too. Maybe Rupa might also chip in with her laptop."

"Great."

As expected, the others were eager to join the task force and soon arrived in the study armed with their laptops. Tara offered to help as well but both Varun and Manu asked her to take charge of Aryan who was being his usual 'helpful' self.

Finally, the promise to charge his iPad made Arya leave the room with Tara. Within an hour, they transformed the study into a control room for coordinating with the various rescue cells, volunteers and also for content creation.

They used Skype and Google Hangouts to make emergency calls and many other online apps to locate people who were still stranded. The status of roads that were submerged was to be updated. They also helped pinpoint the exact location of people who were stranded at various locations using a new app developed by one techie among the volunteers.

It was excruciating work but they did it with a dedication that surprised Manu. Practically they had nothing to gain from this. They were also victims of the flood, but they were doing their best to help others who were stuck in conditions worse than theirs.

At least 325 people had already lost their lives due to severe flooding in Chennai, according to reports. Officials said they expected the death toll to rise once the water levels went down, revealing drowned bodies. It was a very dreary situation.

In truth, they were among the lucky ones. They had not faced hardships like so many others. There were people still marooned in worse conditions. Every one of them needed help.

They were also using social media to announce a list of emergency items that included water bottles, undergarments, sanitary napkins and sleeping mats that were urgently required by the flood victims. They coordinated with multiple NGOs that were stepping in from various parts of India so that help reached the needy as and when needed.

Within hours, they began to receive calls from other volunteers and more work poured in. He had always believed in the fairer side of humanity. The present scenario was the best example that catastrophes brought out the best in humans. People, who were strangers before the disaster struck, were now working together, pooling together their resources to tide over the difficult times. They did not hesitate even for a second to cooperate and strive toward a common good.

Raghu sent another email requesting Manu and Varun to create a short video about the precautions to be taken by those from whose homes flood water had receded. It would have become a breeding ground for diseases and also other venomous creatures like snakes and scorpions must have taken shelter in their homes as well. Reports of people getting bitten by poisonous snakes had also had started coming in.

Manu spent the next hour collecting information about the precautions that needed to be taken and then prepared a script that would make it easy to understand and brief. They would be using images that were being sent by the various volunteers so that they could explain it well using visuals.

As it was already nearing midnight, and plans and programs were in place for the next day, everyone went back to their rooms. Once they left, Varun stretched out on his bed and within minutes, his snores resounded in the room.

Though bone-tired, Manu logged online to check for flight tickets to Bangalore. According to the latest reports, the flights would resume on Sunday, the 5th of December. Partial flight operations were expected to begin tomorrow.

After trying multiple times, he was finally able to book tickets for three on a Monday morning flight. All the earlier flights were already full.

That meant he had just two more days to spend with Tara and Aryan.

25

The next afternoon after lunch, Tara watched as Aryan licked his fingers clean after finishing his share of the *payasam*, the rice porridge. He directed a pleading look at Mary who immediately unloaded another ladle full of payasam on his plate. Though it had been made with milk powder, instead of using fresh milk, it had turned out tasty and Aryan loved it.

Manu, Varun and Pratheesh were playfully competing with him as to who could eat more. Susheela aunty chided the others to let the kid enjoy his share without their interference. The quantity of the payasam, owing to the limited supply of ingredients they had, was less. They had enough, but not enough to fill the tummies of three men who were devouring it as if they were eating the delicious dessert for the first time. Manu had dropped the hint to Mary that Aryan loved payasam while they were all at breakfast. She had immediately set about making it.

Tara sensed that Mary who was sharing her room with Susheela aunty had shared her secret with her. For no reason, Susheela had come up to her in the morning and touched the crown of her head and whispered blessings to 'be loved and prosper'. The only explanation she could think of was that her secret was out.

In fact, she felt, everyone in the group knew.

Aryan was enjoying being pampered by the two elderly ladies. Since morning, they had been taking turns to entertain him with stories. He had told them all about his friends, his schools and of course his cartoons.

"If only my silly son listened to me and got married, I would also have a little hero or heroine to pamper. But who will listen? Even Tarzan had a mate. When will you find your Jane, my Tarzan?" asked Susheela aunty.

"Let me be, Mother India. Live and let live. I love my freedom," replied Varun.

Susheela aunty let out a dramatic sigh and Varun scowled. Aryan, in the meanwhile, was quietly asking Mary for another helping of the porridge.

"Speaking of marriage, when are you guys getting hitched?" Varun asked Pratheesh, cleverly diverting the attention to the couple who were clearly enjoying the unexpected togetherness the floods had given them. If not for the floods, Pratheesh would have been in Delhi for a conference and Rupa would be back in Bangalore managing her art firm.

"We are planning a June wedding. All of you must attend. We won't take no for an answer. The venue will be in Bangalore. Agreed?" asked Pratheesh.

"I'll not miss it for anything," said Varun.

"Yes. We will come," said Manu. Tara too nodded. Her eyes strayed to Manu. He was back to playing fist fights with Aryan. Perhaps that would be when she would be able to see Manu and the others again. The only question was whether she would be able to free herself to attend the marriage.

After lunch, the gang went back to the study, the control room as they now called it, and resumed what they had been doing all along. Manu and Varun had created yet another video and shared it with the public. It was being shared on television channels and news portals on the web to help spread awareness about precautions to be adopted after the flood receded.

Together with the successes, failures also came their way. On multiple instances, volunteers being guided by them to the location as indicated by the last cellular activity of missing persons came across dead bodies.

That night, after Tara tucked Aryan into bed, she wandered onto the terrace to ponder over the many questions that were driving away slumber.

The darkness of the night was still impenetrable. Power had returned but many buildings were still just dark silhouettes in the pale blue of the night. Somehow, the vista reminded her of her future. She didn't expect bright lights and happiness. Yet, she had no one to look up to for help. She was determined to walk the path to help Karthik find the way out of the darkness he had fallen into. She couldn't even imagine the despair he must be going through.

According to Ranjini, Karthik now raged at everyone around or fell into hours of silence. At other times, he acted as if nothing had changed and went back to being his former jovial self. Tara dreaded which persona he was going to take on in front of her.

Another thing that puzzled her was the change she witnessed in Ranjini. Gone were the caustic taunts over the phone or bragging about her blessed life. Whenever Tara called, Ranjini was at the hospital. In fact, Karthik's mother said he listened to only her.

Ranjini was a few months older than Karthik but they had grown up together and were close to each other than Tara ever was to Karthik. For Tara, Karthik was this nerd she could approach to solve perplexing math equations. But for Ranjini, he was the partner in crime. Ranjini was close to most of Karthik's male friends and it was through him that she had met her now-husband, Sridhar. Rupa used to call Ranjini and Karthik the evil twins. No wonder Karthik's accident had mellowed her down.

Someone drummed on the door and she whirled to find Manu standing next to the bedroom door.

Tara's heart skipped a beat. Every time her eyes fell on Manu, a heaviness descended into her chest. She had avoided his presence ever since receiving Karthik's latest update. Manu had instead spent every free moment he had with Aryan. She had watched them from far, fearing that experiencing the bliss they could create together would make it difficult to walk away.

"I have been watching you for the last ten minutes, Tara. It pains me to see you worried. Stop brooding. I told you, I will not demand anything from you. It will be as if you hadn't met me at all."

Tara stared at her own empty hands and swallowed to ease the heaviness she felt in her throat.

"You will forget me, us, all over again. Is that what you are promising?" Tara's voice cracked. She quickly turned away to face the dark horizon again.

She felt him walk near and stop a few feet behind her.

"Would that make things easy for you?" Manu's words were a whisper against her ears. He had moved closer. She could feel his breath on her hair.

She didn't answer. A sob rose and choked her. His heat was creating a cocoon of warmth around her. She wanted to be imprisoned inside it forever.

Manu's breathing had sped up and she felt him press his face against her hair.

"If ..." Manu said softly. The word unleashed a string of wishes that began to unfold inside her rapidly. With a sob, she turned and buried her face in his chest. A flood of 'ifs' tumbled out of her.

"If only I had believed you, Manu. If only I had found out about Aryan before you left. If you had not moved away, we could have been so happy. If..."

Manu shushed her and hugged her tightly.

"What I really want is to throw away the chains society has put on us. I want to be near you and our child. Instead of looking at the virtual memorabilia, you would share with me, I want to create real memories with my child."

Manu held her close and they stayed that way for a long time. Her heart was fluttering like a fish out of water.

"I want all that too. But you know we can't. Even though I do wish we could."

Manu tightened his grip on her arm and pulled her near.

"Do you know how difficult it is to see you inside my house and not touch you?"

Manu's trembling fingers traced her jaw and then grabbed her chin between his forefinger and thumb and directed her gaze to his. His eyes were two intense pools of emotions. Regret, sadness, love and joy. His fingers cupped her head and he dipped his head, closing the distance between their lips.

They had kissed each other a thousand times, and this one kiss shouldn't have felt different. But, it did. Every touch and caress felt deep, pleasure consumed her entire body from lips to toes. It felt like the culmination of something immensely valuable, something she would cherish forever. Tara gave herself over to the kiss, her fingers digging into the silky softness of Manu's hair, then touching his cheeks now rough with stubble.

She could remain like this forever. Tears glittered in her eyes and a few drops flowed down her cheeks. Manu pulled away and gently wiped her tears.

"Don't cry, sweetheart. Your tears make me weak. Nothing can come between us, Tara. As long as my heart beats, I will remain yours. We will not lose each other. I promise you. God will show us the way," said Manu and captured her lips again.

Manu left her after that intense kiss leaving her wondering how she would live without this man beside her. His scent, his voice, his caresses were branded in her memory, yet he would remain just a dream she could hang on to.

26

By Sunday, the floods had receded further. Buses, cars and other vehicles had begun to ply regularly. Rupa, Pratheesh and Ramachandran were preparing to leave by an evening bus to Trivandrum the next day. From there, they would go separate ways. Rupa will return to Bangalore, Ramachandran will stay in Trivandrum and Pratheesh will join his team in Delhi for their new project.

The Bhatts returned from the hospital and were ushered directly to their old room in Manu's house. The Dhananjay who returned from the hospital was a completely different man. He shook hands with all and greeted Susheela aunty and Manu's mother cheerfully. Soumya beamed at everyone and accepted their best wishes.

"I am thrilled to be back. Grateful in fact. The return trip from the verge of death made me appreciate just being alive. But guys... thank you very much. I owe you all my life. Especially you Mr Ramachandran and Mr Manu. Susheela aunty, thank you for your many phone calls."

The atmosphere in the flat was festive. His guests who were planning to leave, Rupa and family, were engaged in packing their things. Dhananjay and Soumya appeared truly happy for the first time since the onset of the floods. Their dreams had changed overnight with the knowledge that a new tiny entity had taken residence in Soumya's womb. They were weaving new dreams. All losses were forgotten.

Everyone was rejoicing at the end of the floods. Except for Manu and Tara. Mother Nature had witnessed them falling in love. She had yet another time thrown them together and helped them undo all their misunderstandings. Yet, they would now part again and face an unknown future.

Manu hadn't let Aryan out of sight all day. Tara had deliberately kept herself out of his way. Every glimpse he got of her was adding to the frustration building inside him. How was he going to live without her?

After lunch, everyone assembled in the living room. It had been Mary who had come up with the idea.

At her behest, Manu had brought down the artificial Christmas tree which they usually set up a week before Christmas. About seven feet tall, the tree had always stood proudly in their living room. Decorating the tree was one of his mother's favourite Christmas rituals.

Together with that, she had asked him to bring down a few other trunks from the overhead lofts in her room. They contained the tree ornaments, fairy lights, gift wrapping paper and whatever a true Christmas celebration called for. This time, she was going to share her joy with her guests. To her, Christmas had come early.

"Sharing gifts is mandatory. As shops haven't reopened yet in the neighbourhood, I want you all to find something or create something for the others. And cards. Handmade cards or letters make all the difference. I want the gifts to be stacked under the tree tonight and we will open them tomorrow morning," Mary said, taking her role as the matron of the gang quite seriously.

They were all happy to comply with her orders.

Aryan was insisting on being part of everything. He walked around the tree inspecting every step of the setting up process. The tree came in parts and was made of plastic. Manu and Varun were in charge of setting it up. Varun was also recording everything.

Mary had packed the tree ornaments after cleaning them thoroughly last year. Yet, she insisted they wipe every ornament clean before it went up on the tree.

Once the tree was set up, she invited Aryan to hang the first ornament. Excited, he selected a golden ball and hung it diligently on one of the branches. He stood back and admired his handiwork and then turned tentatively to check if they all approved. Mary picked him up and planted a loud kiss on his cheeks.

Manu carried him on his shoulders and made him place the golden star, the centrepiece of the decorations on the top of the tree once all decorations were in place. Aryan squealed when Varun switched on the lights and the tree came alive.

Tara, Susheela aunty and Rupa had taken on the duty of preparing a Christmas dinner. They seemed to have become masters at creating food masterpieces out of literally nothing. The dinner turned to be a lavish affair with *Kabuli chana biriyani, dal* fry and *navaratan kuruma along with naan* and *rotis.* Pickles from the Bhatts and Susheela aunty also graced the dining table. Soumya had made a tasty *Kesari bath* for dessert. All in all, it was one of the most memorable dinners Manu had attended in a while. More so because of the company.

To make it more special, they had all dressed up in their best. At Mary's request, a photo session was organised by Varun right in front of the Christmas tree.

The best moment came for Manu when Varun clicked a photo of him with Mary, Tara and Aryan seated together in front of the brightly lit Christmas tree. They looked so perfect together. Complete.

After a while, Mary reminded them all of the promised gifts and handed over stacks of packing paper, scissors and paper to create gifts. Impressed by her perseverance, Manu got up to rummage through his book collection. He chose books to give to everyone except Tara. For her, he wanted to give something special. Something meaningful.

He went up to his room to find the item he had in mind. Aryan's things, including the big red angry bird, had transformed his room from the stark bachelor room into that of a family. It pained him that, within hours, the individuals who had added colour to his drab life would leave. The thought itself was enough to break his heart.

He shook his head and urged himself to do what he had come up to do. He had intended to retrieve a surprise gift he had purchased for Tara five years ago. He hadn't been able to dispose of it even after she broke his heart. He had tucked it away somewhere inside the inner chamber of his wardrobe. Now, it seemed like the best thing he could give her.

He had got the idea when Varun had captured all his loved ones together in one frame, that too in front of the brightly lit Christmas tree. It had come out perfect. In the photo, Aryan was seated on Mary's lap and Tara and Manu had stood behind her. When Varun was about to click the photo, Manu's hands had snaked around Tara's waist and pulled her nearer. Hence, Tara had a shy smile on her face that he hearted. All of them appeared happy. Content. A mirage at best. But the picture had taken on a life of its own the moment it was born. He had wanted it to have a purpose.

After rummaging through the various boxes and files in the inner chamber, he found what he was looking for. A gold chain with an ornate rectangular-shaped pendant. The pendant had a secret chamber that could be opened. Inside, it had a slot to insert photos or messages.

With care, Manu measured the frame inside and returned to the study. After multiple fails, he finally succeeded in printing out the photo on photographic paper in the exact dimensions needed. Within minutes, he had on his palm the perfect Christmas gift.

Gifts are considered to be for the benefit of the receiver. Yet, sometimes, it did the same for the giver as well. Like this memento. He wanted it to constantly remind Tara that they, she and Aryan, belonged here. With him.

Manu wrapped that and the other gifts carefully and labelled them with a marker pen. He packed the Ocean Encyclopedia for Aryan as he'd loved the pictures it contained.

Once the gifts were packed and left beneath the Christmas tree, they got back to the coordination work they had begun. Now SOS calls were very few. The rescue teams had reached every unexplored nook. But still, major work lay ahead. Those who had been forced to leave their flooded homes and those who had lost their homes had to be rehabilitated. Thousands were still living in rescue camps. They needed everything, starting from the basic necessities. Students who had lost their books needed them replaced. Important real estate documents and certificates that had been lost had to be replaced.

Manu sat discussing this with Varun and Dhananjay while Aryan sat on his lap playing games on Tara's phone. Rupa and her family had retired to their rooms to pack.

"Daddy..." screamed Aryan suddenly. He then hugged Manu and kissed him on his cheek. Wide-eyed and his heart thudding, Manu kissed him back. He had longed so much to hear Aryan call him that way. "See, it is Daddy's name. I thought he was angry with me," Aryan explained as he swiped the answer icon on the phone which was ringing.

The whole room fell silent. Tara was playing with the knots on her shawl.

"I am fine. Yes, Mummy is fine too. We are coming home tomorrow morning. How are you, Daddy? I missed you too."

Manu mentally chided himself for feeling jealous. But still, the jealousy monster poked his long and sharp fingers straight into his heart. The innocent talk of his son was making him aware that he was not part of his little world. The part he wished to play was already being enacted by another person. He would never replace Karthik. Truth felt like a bitter and sour soup. After a while, Aryan gave the phone to Tara and she walked out of the room to speak with Karthik.

Aryan's happiness was reflected on his face. Manu felt grateful to Karthik. His son didn't experience the lack of a father figure in his life. Unlike him, Aryan's father seemed to have loved him and spent quality time with him.

Aryan would remember him, his biological father, as a stranger with whom he had spent a few fun moments. He would never even suspect that Manu, that stranger, was his father.

When Tara returned to the room after talking with Karthik, she gestured at Manu to follow her and walked out of the room. Wordlessly he followed.

Tara was waiting for him on the terrace.

"What is it, Tara?"

"Manu, I couldn't tell Karthik that we were with you. I just couldn't do it. He is eager to see us back. I lied to him that we are staying with a family known to Aparna. You shouldn't accompany us tomorrow. It will raise a lot of questions."

Manu had expected something of this sort. But he did not want to agree to her request.

"I am coming with you tomorrow to Bangalore. But I won't come to the hospital. Allow me to see you both back safely to Bangalore, Tara. It will give me a few more hours to be with you."

Tara nodded and then quickly walked away. Pain stabbed his heart, as it did every time he saw Tara walking away from him. He had heard that love doesn't understand its own depth until the final hour of separation. Until the agony of parting clenched it with its iron grip. Now he could comprehend it completely.

27

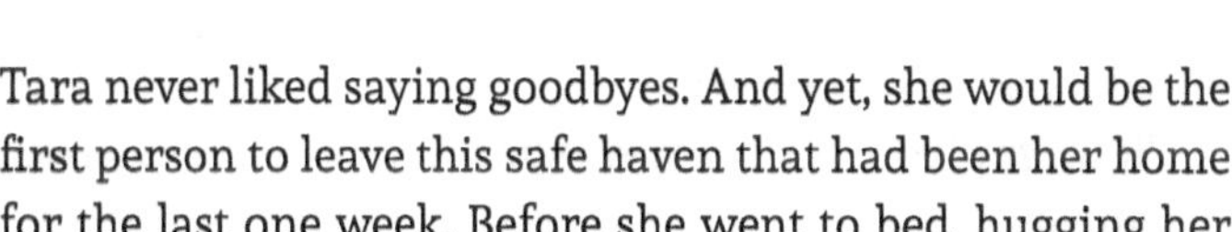

Tara never liked saying goodbyes. And yet, she would be the first person to leave this safe haven that had been her home for the last one week. Before she went to bed, hugging her tight Rupa had repeated her earlier advice that Tara should return to Manu.

Tara had no idea how she could do that. Her life at the moment was a tangled mess. Manu would continue to be her despair. But this time she was taking back with her memories that would be oxygen to her during her moments of despair.

In the morning, Aryan had been the first to wake up. He had woken up multiple times in the night to inquire if *'it was morning yet?'* At the first sign of morning, he had run down to the Christmas tree to search for his gift. Once there, he found out he was not the only one who had come down. All of the others were up as well.

Susheela aunty, Soumya and Rupa came from the kitchen with filter coffee for everyone. They all settled down on the couch and chairs to open their gifts.

Aryan was digging through the pile of gifts with Manu's help. He counted ten packets that had his name written on them. Tara was surprised to see that she got ten gifts too. Everyone had found something to gift to each member of the gang. Including Aryan, they were eleven in number.

Aryan screamed with glee when he found two more extra gifts bearing his name. Mary and Manu both had given him two gifts each. Manu's gifts were a book about the ocean he had loved and a DVD about the different kinds of birds in India. Mary had given him a blue sweater with a pretty A embroidered on it. She had knitted it for Aryan spending hours on it daily ever since she knew he was her grandson. The second gift from her was a box of chocolates. After opening each box, Aryan ran to the person who had gifted it and hugged them.

"Mummy, you should open your gifts as well," insisted Aryan.

"No, Aryan. We have to get ready, remember? Don't you want me to pack all your gifts?"

Aryan was in no mood to obey Tara but Varun came in and distracted him by asking him to pose for some new snaps. Ever the eager model, Aryan immediately started striking poses.

Once back in the room, Tara fished out what Mary had given her first. Inside the gift packet, she found a note.

"I never got a chance to gift you anything. I hope you will like this. Thank you for giving me a reason to hope."

Mary.

She had gifted her a green, silk saree. It looked brand new.

Tara opened the gifts from everyone leaving the present from Manu to be opened last. Everyone had chosen apt gifts for her. Rupa had gifted her a paperback thriller. Soumya had gifted her a journal. Dhananjay and Pratheesh had given her pens. Varun had given her a CD with photos from their stay here and Susheela aunty had given her a silk shawl.

She had gifted copies of her book to all except Manu. She had received ten copies from Aparna. For Manu, she had copied all the videos and photos she had on her computer to a USB. She had a habit of recording Aryan's videos right from childhood. She had uploaded only the best on her website. This was the only thing she could do to give him a glimpse into Aryan's growing years. She had promised him in the note enclosed to continue writing to him via the blog. She planned to upload more photos and videos.

Finally, with trepidation, she opened the gift box Manu had given. She recognised the gift immediately and her heart began a happy dance.

She had found this pendant in an antique jewellery shop in Kannur all those years ago. That afternoon, she had asked Manu's help to get a bracelet gifted by her grandmother repaired. It had lost the screw that had held it in place. While they waited, Tara had found an interesting pendant on the display wall of the jewellery shop. A pendant that had a secret chamber. She had loved it at sight. As it came with a gold chain, even though she had loved it, she had kept it back. She had talked about it non-stop on their way back.

Manu must have gone back alone to purchase it for her. And he had kept it safe all these years. While her heart thudded in excitement, she opened the pendant to check what Manu had put inside.

The photo of them together made her heart grow warm and her eyes misted. In addition, Manu had put a tiny scroll inside as well. It simply said, *'Remember, we love you.'*

She placed a kiss on the pendant and then unclasped it intending to wear it. While she was struggling to clasp it, she heard footsteps. Turning around, she found the man who had gifted it standing in the doorway.

Wordlessly, Manu came to help her. After pushing her hair out of the way, he tied the necklace around her neck. Turning her around, he admired his gift that now adorned her. Tara felt her cheek grow warm when his gaze fell to her lips. As he leaned near, Tara closed her eyes anticipating a kiss. The moment was broken when a merry voice sounded in the room.

"Mummy, what all gifts did you get? Show them all to me." While Aryan started to sift through her gifts, Tara played with the pendant. Manu's eyes were intense. Was he feeling the pang of separation the way she was feeling already?

She was a master at pretending, having aced it because of experience. She smiled at Manu cheerfully and thanked him for the gift. Then she addressed Aryan and started stuffing the gifts into her bag. At that moment, Varun called Aryan and Aryan ran out of the room to check what his hero was doing next.

The moment Aryan moved out of the room, Manu grabbed Tara and pulled her into his arms. "Promise me you will give us a chance," he whispered before devouring her mouth. He pressed her palm on his chest as he deepened the kiss. She could feel the soft thud of his heart against her palm. Tara returned the kiss, as her hand snaked around his back, bunching his shirt into her fingers.

Manu pulled her tighter towards him and then trailed kisses down her cheek and throat. With a groan, he buried his face in her bosom. Tara melted. She wished more. Desire thrummed through her veins as Manu's hand wandered around her body.

At the sound of Aryan running up the stairs, Tara gently pushed Manu away and moved away from his arms. Manu looked tortured. She sighed and looked away.

Manu was at the door when Aryan rushed in again.

"Have you kept everything in your bag? We have to leave in an hour. Be ready, okay?" Manu said to Aryan as he bent down to fist bump his son."Is there anything else you want from here?"

Aryan kept his forefinger on his cheek and then addressed him, "Can we take Grandma with us? I want to show her my storybooks."

"We can't. We don't have tickets for her. But I promise I will bring her to Bangalore when we come for Rupa aunty's marriage."

Continuing their chatter, Manu lifted Aryan and walked down to the living room, with Aryan perched on his shoulders. This was Aryan's favourite way of travelling around the house now. Whenever they were together, he insisted he wanted to be carried on his shoulder.

She would miss all this. In the last two days, she had got glimpses of how life could truly be if she chose to be with Manu. But how could she choose Manu when the one who truly required her now was Karthik? She would surely regret her decision for sure but perhaps this was how it was meant to be.

Karthik's accident was a reminder that she shouldn't dream much. Hers was a cursed incarnation. Perhaps she was paying for her sins from a past life.

Being literature students, they had once been asked to write about their thoughts about reincarnation. She believed in reincarnation. It made perfect sense and explained why things happened in a certain way. Rich people lost all their wealth one day without any warning. Lovers parted and went different ways. Some human beings arrived on earth with only despair written in their destiny. It seemed like the most believable explanation. Or did the ancients use Karma to keep men from straying onto dangerous paths?

That was the question that kept looping in her mind throughout their journey to Bangalore.

When Manu bid goodbye to them after seating them in a prepaid airport taxi, Tara surreptitiously wiped the tears that had tumbled out from her eyes.

Please God, make him happy. That was the only prayer that Tara repeated while she gazed at him in the rear-view mirror as their car moved away. She knew where his happiness lay. But she had no way to grant him that happiness. It was her biggest regret.

28

Six months later

The sound of flowing water assured him that Tara was still in the bathroom. Karthik quickly kept the necklace back in her jewellery box. He had pried open the necklace and the photo inside had clarified his doubts.

He had seen Tara happy after weeks yesterday. Truly happy. The reason had been Rupa's visit.

Rupa had come to invite them to her marriage along with her fiancé, Pratheesh. Upon seeing them, Tara had become a changed person. It was as if she had suddenly bloomed again. He had rejoiced that Rupa had accomplished doing what he had failed to do in months.

Then, after they had left, when she thought nobody was watching, he had found her pressing her lips on the pendant. It was as if their arrival had reminded her of the person who had gifted it to her. His curiosity about it had been piqued. Tara wore the chain always and she had acquired it after her stay in Chennai. Upon enquiry, she had said it had been a Christmas gift from the family she had been staying with.

In the weeks following her return from Chennai, he had attributed her silence and moodiness to his accident. After all, their life had been turned upside down. But he soon came to realize that was not the case. Something had happened in Chennai. What, he had no idea. Then it had slipped from Rupa's fiance' how time had flown and they hadn't been able to meet even once after their time together in Chennai. Though Karthik had wanted to pursue it, Tara had quickly changed the topic of conversation.

Curious, he had turned to social media to find more. As he had been in the hospital at the time, he had not been able to know much about the Chennai floods. Often, tragedies made people active on social media. Either to help others or to request help. So, he had snooped on the Facebook timelines of Rupa and Pratheesh during the time of the floods.

Rupa had only posted requests about donating essential goods for the flood victims and many SOS messages. But on Pratheesh's timeline, he came across a video by a famous YouTuber Varun Chinnappa. Aryan's face in the thumbnail of the video made him click on the video link. The video told him all he wanted to know when a few minutes into the recording, Manu appeared on the screen explaining the easiest way to create a rain-catcher. It seemed they had been together all those days.

Karthik had sat frozen in his wheelchair unable to move a single finger. What a cruel twist of fate! On the day that he had threatened Tara to return to his life as his wife, she had met with Manu. How convenient for them that the floods had thrown them together. How convenient that he was now a vegetable. Anger and frustration flooded his being.

He began to look out for signs of infidelity from Tara. But he couldn't find anything. No sneaky phone calls, no long hours of absence. Nothing. The only difference was that it seemed like Tara was losing the light in her eyes day after day. It was like she had lost interest to live.

His psychologist arranged by the hospital still came in weekly to counsel him about his new life. His limited mobility had not succeeded to snub his enthusiasm. He was slowly becoming accustomed to being this person who would never move anywhere without the help of another person. Though bound to his wheelchair, he had become determined to not become a burden to anyone. Especially to Tara.

And then Rupa's invitation had come. Tara had come back to life. In the past twenty-four hours, she had returned to being the girl he had fallen in love with. The girl for whom he would do anything. And the painful realization had dawned. That perhaps the prospect of meeting Manu again was the reason for her happiness.

Six months ago, after he had regained consciousness, his first and foremost wish had been to see Tara and Aryan. The accident had been horrible. But to his dismay, they were stuck in Chennai which was reeling under the floods.

"Can you see me, Karthik?" The doctor had asked after being seated in front of him. When he nodded, he had grabbed his right arm.

"Can you feel my touch?"

"Of course," he had said with slight irritation wishing the checkup to be over finally. He wanted to slip back into the dreamless sleep till he was fully healed. He'd had enough from visiting relatives, friends, and colleagues. He just wanted to be left alone. The only face he wanted to see was miles away. He had no idea when she would return.

"Can you try and move your toes, Karthik?" the doctor had asked.

'Of course," he had said. To his horror, his body had simply refused to listen to his command. However much he tried, he couldn't move his lower body.

The doctor had patted his hand and asked him to relax.

"What is wrong with me, doctor?" he had asked, fear piercing him with its steel tentacles. The doctor's words had left him shaken. The accident had severely damaged his spinal cord. He was paralyzed below his hips. Not just for weeks, but forever.

Ranjini who had been beside him had shuddered and grabbed his arm. Was this God's way of telling him he had erred? He had seen the same question reflected in her eyes as well.

In the days that followed while he waited for Tara to arrive, he had been counselled by the in-house counsellor at the hospital. He had seen videos from around the world about young people like him who shared his condition.

Once the initial despair had worn off, he had decided to follow the examples of the hundreds of other paraplegics he had met through the various forums he had found online. With their help, he had found comfort in the fact that he was still alive.

The MNC he was working for was extremely helpful and he had been awarded a slightly lower grade work-from-home post. They didn't want to let go of a brilliant employee like him. It had been the dose of hope that he had needed. The fact that he was now frozen below his hips did not bother him much. His enthusiasm that he would find a way to make everything work had been going uphill until that day Rupa came.

From then on, he had transformed into a spy. He watched Tara like an eagle, his possessive streak raising its head. Yet he had found nothing that caused him to worry. She had retreated into a shell. She had cancelled her book launch functions in Delhi and the one in Bangalore stating his condition. Her book had become a bestseller already but he didn't see her writing anymore. It was as if she was falling into depression yet again.

He had seen her through it once. And he was determined to do it again. He attended his counselling sessions and physiotherapy sessions with a rigour that would have put even military generals to shame. He laughed, entertained his friends and even bought a modified car for paraplegics. Nothing would stop him from living his life. And he would make Tara believe in him again.

It didn't take him long to realize that Tara was not his anymore. She was trying hard to be the loving wife that she was before. But he found her every morning with eyes swollen red and dark circles around her eyes gifted by grief and sleepless nights.

True, even for a moment she hadn't made him feel that he was a burden to her. Even before he asked, he found the things he needed. His meals reached the dining table on time. His guests were received with a smile. Yet, it wasn't enough.

Pressing the move button on his wheelchair, he manoeuvred himself away from Tara's room. He returned to the living room and found Rupa's marriage invitation. The wedding was still a week away. Taking out his phone, he called Ranjini and asked her to meet him at a nearby wheelchair friendly restaurant. And he waited for Tara to return after her bath.

It took a herculean effort to convince Tara to let him go alone. But his arguments were strong. He was already an expert in using his car. And the restaurant was just a few blocks away.

"Call me when you reach there," Tara surrendered finally.

"I will, sweetheart," he said and rolled his wheelchair out of their home. It was about time to pick Aryan from school. That had been another reason that Tara had agreed to let him go alone. He felt her gaze on him when he reversed the car from their garage and easily moved onto the road. His new modified car was easy to drive and with his former expertise, it had not been much of an effort to learn to drive it.

Ranjini met him at the restaurant entrance and then accompanied him to the table that he had pre-booked. Once they settled, Karthik gulped down the glass of water the waiter had filled just then and dived right into the topic.

"Manu is back in Tara's life," he said, crushing a tissue he had picked up from the table.

"How did you know?" Ranjini asked.

Her question stunned him. A million questions ran through his mind. Did she know about it? Had she chosen to hide it from him? How could she? Had Tara told her? What was the status of their relationship?

"Tara told you? Why didn't you tell me? Or were you allowing your sister to cuckold me?"

"Relax. There is no need to go hyper about it. I came to know about it accidentally. A friend forwarded a WhatsApp video that had gone viral during the Chennai floods asking if the kid in the video was my nephew. I was stunned to see Aryan with Manu."

"When was this? And why didn't you tell me?"

"For God's sake Karthik, you were recovering from your accident. I didn't want to burden you with more heartache. You had enough on your plate already. Do you think I would have wished that on you?"

"So, you chose to keep mum," said Karthik.

"Of course, I did not keep mum. I confronted her."

Karthik waited with bated breath to hear his worst fears confirmed.

"Nothing happened between them if that is what you fear. They lived in the same house. But there were others with them."

He quickly took out his phone and scrolled through it till he found what he was looking for. Tara with Manu and his mother in front of a Christmas tree. Jealousy had conquered him completely when he had found the photo inside the pendant. Tara had never appeared this happy and content in any of their family portraits. But this one looked perfect.

"This doesn't seem like nothing. They look like a happy family, damn it," he said handing the mobile to Ranjini.

"Where did you find it?" Ranjini asked. She seemed clearly taken aback.

"Inside the pendant of the chain that she wears 24/7. It's his gift. I am sure. I can't believe Tara cheated on me," said Karthik.

"No. She didn't. She assured me that all she did was apologise to him for what happened years ago. And she told him about Aryan," said Ranjini.

"She told him about Aryan? I am not a fool to believe that Manu would let his child live with me after knowing the truth. I will kill him if he slams a court notice on me," Karthik said. Why hadn't he received a notice from Manu's lawyers already? Didn't he want to stake a claim on his son?

"Not everyone thinks as you do, Karthik. I thought this accident might have toned you down. No. You are still the same heartless bastard who doesn't think twice before manipulating people to suit his own needs."

"Look who is speaking! Have you forgotten everything already? I am not half as cruel as you. I loved Tara. I did it out of love for her."

Ranjini had met Sridhar, who had been Karthik's acquaintance, at a party they had attended together. They had hit it off and soon they were committed. When Ranjini came to know about Tara's love affair, she had approached Karthik to ask for help. Hatred had consumed him when he learned that the girl he loved was in love with another. He had taken steps to save her from committing a huge mistake.

"Out of love? Really? Fine. I did it to protect my marriage. My would-be-in-laws would have cancelled my engagement with Sridhar if Tara married a Christian boy. They are very orthodox in their beliefs."

"So, you approached me, clearly knowing that I loved Tara. I would have gone to any lengths to keep her to myself. Like a fool, I agreed to help you."

"You are a fool when it comes to her. Can't you see that she will never be yours? She loved that boy and would always love him. When will you realize that? Your plan to separate them worked once. But did you succeed in making her love you? She is yours only on paper."

Karthik felt the blood rushing into his face. It hurt because she was saying the truth. She laughed.

"Truth hurts, doesn't it? But Karma is a bitch. Isn't it strange that you met with that accident the day they reunited?"

Kartik wished he could strangle Ranjini. He would have perhaps done that if not for the sudden change that came over Ranjini.

Ranjini seemed to have frozen in her seat. Her eyes had opened wide, as if in shock. Something had caught her eye. Following her line of sight, Karthik found what she'd seen.

In a sheltered corner in the room, Sridhar, Ranjini's husband, was at lunch with his secretary. Their body language screamed that their relationship was not professional at all. Sridhar was feeding her pieces of meat he picked from his plate. They didn't seem to care about anything or anyone around them.

"How dare he! He has taken this too far. The bastard." Ranjini's features distorted, first with shock and then with anger. Grabbing the glass of water from her table, she approached the happy couple and splashed it right onto them. Expletives that had emanated from Sridhar's mouth froze when he recognised Ranjini.

Sridhar must have never expected Ranjini inside this restaurant. She never ate in restaurants that had fewer than five stars in their description. This nondescript restaurant being near Sridhar's office must have been his regular haunt.

Unfortunately, the cat was out of the bag. Karma was indeed a bitch.

29

Tara fiddled with her pendant again. The auditorium was slowly filling with people. She glanced around checking for the presence of Manu or Mary. Hadn't they arrived yet? Maybe it would be better if they didn't come.

She had been looking forward to it all week. She had worn the saree Mary had gifted. The home nurse had been given clear instructions as to what Karthik needed. But there hadn't been any need. Karthik had insisted that he wished to accompany her. After all, Rupa had invited them both. She hadn't been able to message Manu to not come as her phone had suddenly gone missing from her bedside table. She clearly remembered leaving it for charging.

Karthik had contacted Pratheesh who had informed them that the hall was wheelchair friendly. His grandma was now wheelchair-bound. Hence he had gone to all lengths to assure that she could attend the marriage.

Tara was in awe of Karthik. She would have been devastated if she had been the victim of such an accident. But Karthik had taken full control of his life all over again. He had insisted that only a male home nurse tends to him when he needed. The middle-aged man they had found was just perfect for his needs. He lived just a few blocks away and came in whenever they called.

Tara glanced around nervously and then headed to the dressing room where Rupa was getting ready. Maybe she could borrow her phone and warn Manu. She didn't want Karthik to be upset.

All her hopes vanished when Mary greeted her warmly when she entered the dressing room. Aryan was over the moon with happiness and gave Mary a sloppy kiss on her cheeks. Mary picked him up and asked Tara how she was doing.

Manu was with Pratheesh, Mary told her. In the men's dressing room. Tara's legs trembled in panic. That was where Karthik had gone. He had said he wanted to meet the groom and wish him before the rituals began.

Leaving Aryan with Mary, Tara scampered out of the female dressing room. With her heart pounding against her ribs, she darted towards the men's dressing room.

She pushed open the men's dressing room ready to face anything.

"Just the woman I wanted to see," exclaimed Karthik on seeing her. Manu and Pratheesh were the only other occupants of the room. What was happening? Manu smiled at her and so did Pratheesh.

"Look who I found, Tara! I hope you remember Manu," Karthik said.

Tara's fingers flew towards the pendant subconsciously. She covered it with her palm as if by doing so she could protect Manu.

The silence that filled the room was disturbing. Did Karthik come to know somehow that she had met Manu in Chennai? But only Ranjini knew. Did her sister betray her yet another time?

Tara felt sweat drops beading on her forehead.

"Hello, Tara. How are you?" asked Manu, clearly trying to keep up appearances. His voice sounded like the sweetest sound in the world to her.

"I am fine," Tara said softly. She was not fine. Not at all. Any moment she expected Karthik to start accusing her of being unfaithful to him. But to her relief, nothing happened. He politely enquired what Manu was up to these days.

Then after shaking Pratheesh's hand, Karthik moved out of the room.

Manu's eyes met hers and the warmth of his presence washed over her. Yet, within moments all her fears returned. Would Karthik suspect anything? Was he upset?

She returned to where Rupa was and forced herself to appear cheerful. Rupa was looking beautiful in her red bridal saree. She had selected traditional ornaments that were elegant and beautiful. Her hair was adorned with jasmines and an artificial braid with attached ornaments completed the look.

Tara wanted to discuss with Rupa what had just happened but now was not the time. She couldn't add this to her nerves. Many more known faces came to greet Tara including Dhananjay, Soumya, Susheela aunty, Varun and Ramachandran. A few of Rupa's relatives who knew Tara also came to greet Tara and make small talk.

Rupa became Mrs Pratheesh within the next half an hour and people started queuing up to meet and greet the newlyweds and pose for group photographs. To Tara's surprise, when she got down from the stage and sought Aryan, she found him seated on Manu's lap, sitting next to Karthik.

Mary's face was blank and devoid of any emotion as she appeared to be listening to something Karthik was eagerly telling her. Tara pinched herself to check if she was dreaming. This was beyond her wildest dreams. Any moment, she feared Karthik would turn to her and raise an accusing finger.

Her eyes met Manu's and she searched his face to see for any signs of unease. Nothing. Perhaps, this storm would pass without unravelling the tapestry of her life which already had so many tangled threads.

The impasse continued throughout lunch. By now though, Mary had become an admirer of Karthik. Mary's face was filled with sympathy. She was praising Karthik's courage and his determination not to give up.

Once lunch got over, Karthik invited Mary and Manu to their home. Their flight was not until evening. Tara wasn't sure if it was a good idea. But Mary readily agreed.

So thus, within an hour, Tara found Manu sitting in her living room calmly conversing with Karthik.

While she made coffee for them, her thoughts raced. Manu appeared calm outwardly. The pain must be gnawing at him on the inside. He was in her world, the world in which his presence was an aberration.

Aryan had dragged Mary along with him, to his room. Tara heard his giggles while she transferred coffee into the various cups. After finding a few biscuits to go along with it, she arranged the plates and cups in a tray and carried them into the living room. Manu was going through some papers that Karthik had given to him. Were they his medical papers? And why was he showing them to Manu? It seemed strange.

Upon seeing her, Karthik came toward her and picked a cup of coffee from her tray.

"I was showing Manu our divorce agreement," said Karthik and the tray wobbled in her hands. What did he say? Divorce agreement? When had she agreed to a divorce?

Manu appeared equally stupefied by what he was reading. Grabbing the papers from his hand, she looked through them. It was indeed a divorce agreement. There it was, hers and Karthik's sign at the bottom to prove it. They had agreed to a mutual divorce. Nothing made sense.

"It was an out of the court settlement. Strictly carried over in secrecy. We wanted it that way. Am I wrong, Tara?"

Tara glared at Karthik. What sort of game was he playing?

"What is this nonsense? When did I sign these papers?" Then it came to her. Karthik had made her sign a bunch of papers that were necessary to claim his insurance according to him. She had read through the initial papers but Karthik had hurried her through. These papers must have been somehow inserted between them.

"You cheated me to get them signed. I can't believe you did that. What are you planning to accomplish with that? If you didn't want me in your life, you could have told me that. There was no need to play this drama. There was no need to drag Manu into all this."

"Says the girl who has been enacting the role of being my loving wife all these years. Are you not tired of it, Tara? I am sick of it. I married you because I loved you. But you were never mine. You belonged and still belong to that man sitting there. I was a fool to think that if I succeeded in separating you two, you would become mine."

Karthik swallowed as if he had accidentally said something that he was not supposed to say.

"What do you mean? You separated us?" Tara paused to comprehend what she had just heard before resuming. "Now I get it. You were Ranjini's accomplice in plotting Manu's downfall. I had always wondered how Ranjini came up with such a nefarious plot. But that was your plan, right? Your lawyer brain wouldn't have had much difficulty in coming up with such a deceptive plot. You could have easily found a prostitute."

Manu had got up from his seat, his face crimson.

"I have loved you for so long. But you always thought of me like the brother you never had. Even Ranjini. She was my partner in crime even though I would have preferred you to become mine. I am not ashamed of what I did. I did it all entirely for love," Karthik said, without even a tinge of shame.

A slap sounded and Karthik cupped his cheek and looked up at Mary's face, which was blazing with anger.

"So, you were the monster who destroyed my son's life? I feel ashamed to think that Manu gave up his own son to keep you happy. But this plight you are in is proof that there is a God above who watches over us. You deserve everything that you went through. You never got the girl you love and you will never will."

Though she wanted to do exactly what Mary had done, Tara tugged Mary away from Karthik's vicinity. She willed herself to remain calm.

How had she not seen through his plans? And she had prepared to sacrifice everything for this man. She had prepared to forget the man she loved. She had rejected Manu's offer of love yet another time.

But still, one thing puzzled her. What had made him act out this elaborate drama to bring Manu and her together? Because in hindsight, that was exactly what he had done. He had gone out of the way to lure them to his house and then assured Manu that Tara was free from his clutches.

Karthik appeared to have expected this. Manu had picked up Aryan when Mary had lashed out at Karthik.

He had walked out of the house carrying him as he was insisting on climbing onto Karthik's lap to kiss him alright.

"Why Karthik? Answer me." Tara stepped in front of Karthik.

"I give up, Tara. I can't do this anymore. I already have to fight with this body of mine to just survive. I don't want you to be my crutch. I wrote this destiny for myself. As Mary rightly said, this is my karma. You don't deserve to be punished for my mistakes. I still love you, Tara. I can't see you dying right in front of my eyes. Every day I am losing a bit of the Tara I once loved. And I am done playing this farce." Karthik's face shone with determination.

Tara looked at him speechlessly. She couldn't believe what she was hearing. Was this a trap of some sort?

"I want you to be gone from this house before morning. You are no longer my wife." Karthik's voice boomed in the living room.

"I don't want to spend another moment under your roof. I hate you, Karthik," Tara snapped at him. Karthik's lips curled in a smirk.

"Isn't that just what the doctor prescribed? I won't allow my grandson to live under the shadow of your evil presence. Your deception ends now. Come on, Tara, pack your bags. You will come with us."

Tara followed Mary and began packing her things. A while later, Karthik's screams sounded from his bedroom. Tara threw the clothes she had been tucking into her suitcase on the bed and rushed out fearing the worst. Was Manu taking out his anger on Karthik?

Her fear was proved wrong when she saw Manu rushing in through the front door carrying Aryan. He also had heard the screams.

When they reached Karthik's room, Tara tried the door. It was locked. Putting Aryan down, Manu prepared to force the door open by force as no sound came from the room now. Mary stopped him.

"Knowing how evil he can be, I don't think that is a prudent step. Call the police."

Tara had to agree with Mary's logic. Knowing Karthik, anything could await them on the other side of the door.

It took another half hour for the police to arrive. When they forced the bedroom door open, they found Karthik dead in his wheelchair.

He had electrocuted himself to death by holding onto a steel wire inserted into a plug. A suicide note lay on the bed accusing Manu and Tara of driving him to take this extreme step. He accused Tara of infidelity and for forcing him to agree to a divorce with huge alimony. As proof, he stated that Manu was the biological father of Aryan.

Knowing Karthik, he must have planned everything to the last detail.

Every single thing that happened during the day made sense.

They were in so much trouble.

30

Three months later

Manu fondly gazed at the beautiful girl walking down the aisle towards him. Dressed in an off-white silk saree with gold zari work, hair gathered in an updo, with a tiara holding her veil in place, she looked like a dream. His eyes misted and he surreptitiously wiped away a drop that had slipped out. It was their wedding day.

Aryan, who was the official ring bearer, stood proudly on the stage watching his mother. Manu and Aryan were dressed in identical formal black suits. Pratheesh, his best man was right beside him. Rupa was Tara's maid of honour. He could see many friendly, smiling faces gazing up at them.

Varun was their official wedding photographer. Manu and Varun had become close friends after what Varun had done for him and Tara in the past three months. He had been their pillar of support along with Rupa and Pratheesh.

The pain and humiliation that he had endured way back in college had seemed like nothing compared to what he and Tara went through in the months after Karthik's death.

Karthik had also mailed his suicide note to the media before he took his life. Manu and Tara were arrested and put behind bars for abetting suicide after his relatives filed a police complaint. The public ire towards them had been fueled like an inferno with the media hounding them daily after they got out on bail.

Everything had seemed to go downhill until help came from an unexpected quarter. Ranjini who had been Karthik's secret keeper all along had recorded all their conversations. In one of them, they were discussing how years ago they had together managed to separate Manu and Tara. In another, he was bragging how he had stealthily got Tara's signature on an out-of-court divorce agreement.

"If Tara can't be mine, she won't belong to anyone." That had been Karthik's exact words. His ultimate aim.

Ranjini who was facing trouble in her own marriage had begun to believe that it was her bad Karma that was beginning to blight the light in her life.

Together with that, Varun who had been their main public voice of support throughout the crisis created a video chronicling their love story. It went viral on social media. Suddenly, they had become the darlings of the masses. With the court ruling in their favour very soon, luck had started to smile on them.

After all the pain they had endured, their friends had insisted to make it the most memorable event even though they would have been happy with a low-key court marriage. Mary, who had always dreamed about his marriage, persisted till they agreed to celebrate their wedding in the way she wished.

Mary had taken full responsibility for planning a wedding that would truly begin their life together. Rupa and Pratheesh had taken the prospective bride and groom dress shopping claiming they knew just the right places to find practically everything they needed.

Karthik's malice had opened the eyes of Tara's parents as well. They had welcomed Manu into their family with happiness. Now Tara's father was escorting Tara down the aisle while her mother was wiping silent tears.

Ranjini was conspicuous by her absence. She was travelling and had conveyed her greetings to them today morning. She didn't want to be part of the wedding festivities. Not when she was preparing for a dirty legal battle. She had filed for divorce accusing her husband of cheating and infidelity.

Manu gazed at Tara who had by now reached near him.

"You look so beautiful, Tara," he whispered. Her answer was a shy smile.

Manu was looking forward to spending a lifetime together with this cheerful, bubbly girl he had fallen in love with. It didn't matter that they had lost five years of their life waiting for this moment to arrive. The delay had only resulted in increasing the ardour they shared. It was a love that they often had thought not possible and the way it had returned to them after having almost lost each other, not once but twice, made it all the more precious.

Tara had started writing again. Words had begun to flow even while they were in the middle of vitriolic attacks from the media. She had used her blog to tell her story, to make herself heard in the din. Her books had begun to sell like hotcakes thanks to the interest sparked by the media scandal and the court case.

The officiant cleared his throat and began.

"Friends and family, we are gathered here today..."

The officiant, a vicar who was a family friend, gave a small speech about the significance of the vows they were about to exchange, the sanctity of marriage and reminded the bride and groom about the duties and roles in marriage.

Once they exchanged their vows, Aryan, who had declared that he was a big boy already, and acting like one today, brought the rings on cue from Pratheesh.

Picking up the wedding ring, Manu looked into Tara's eyes." With this ring, I thee wed," he said as he slid the ring on Tara's left ring finger.

"With this ring, I thee wed," repeated Tara while making him wear the ring.

Pratheesh handed him the *thali*, the traditional wedding chain, a golden chain with a leaf-shaped pendant, popular among South Indian Christians. Sending up gratitude to the heavenly father, Manu tied the chain around Tara's neck.

Next, he handed over the *manthrakodi*, the traditional wedding saree, to Tara.

Immediately after, the officiant blessed them and declared them husband and wife. To add to the fun, he declared,

"You may now kiss the bride."

Manu was ready to comply when a tiny, yet loud voice declared.

"I don't want to see that. Kissing is gross." Aryan's words threw the audience into splits.

Aryan had turned away and hidden his face with his hands to avoid watching them kiss.

Chuckling, Manu picked up Aryan and kissed both his cheeks. Thankfully, he had no problem when his new Daddy kissed him instead. Manu pulled Tara near and kissed her cheeks as well.

His heart thudded contently when Mary, after blessing them, entered into the happy circle of his arms.

This was all he needed, all he had ever dreamed about.

His tiny world was finally complete.

-The end

Author's Note

Reviews matter to the success of any book.

If you liked this story, please leave a review on the Amazon page of the book.

You can write to me also: authorpreethi@gmail.com.

Regards,

Preethi Venugopala

Acknowledgements

This was a very difficult story to write mostly because of the theme. Another reason was that it is based in Chennai. I am not a Chennaite.

I started writing the story of Tara and Manu after the floods hit Chennai. After writing the first few chapters, I abandoned the manuscript because I didn't feel I could do justice to it. Then the floods hit Kerala, my home state, in 2018, and the horror of the situation hit me again. Tara and Manu's story began to take shape once again.

I have many friends living in Chennai and I was worried about their safety and well-being during the floods. As it always happens, the stories I heard from them began to make their way into the manuscript as well.

I have many of my friends to thank for the story.

Thank you, Arvind Sampath, Nita Anand, Kirthi Jayakumar, Chithra Mohan, Radhika Jayaraman and Sudha Nair for the valuable inputs you gave about the flood situation in Chennai.

Thank you, Dhivya Balaji, for your incisive beta reading and feedback. Dhivya is a Chennai resident and had faced the floods in all its horror. Her inputs gave depth to this story. If any error in details has crept in, it is entirely my fault.

Thank you, Nikita Jhanglani, my editor, for your razor-sharp editing and valuable input. As I always tell you, you are a gem.

A big thank you to my husband Venugopala and my son Akshaj who were my role models for Manu and Aryan in this book. I hope they like how I have portrayed them.

My mother, Panchali is the one who never ends her call without asking me how my writing is going. I thank her for being my pillar of support.

My siblings, Dr Sunil Kannada and Dr Mini Kannada are always there to clear my medical doubts. I thank them for their input and for being a positive presence in my life.

My writing life is made colourful by the presence of a group of bubbly individuals called writing buddies. I thank all of you, my dear friends, for egging me on with writing sprints and word counts. You know who you are.

If not for the magician called Google, I might not have been able to complete this book. Thank you, Google, for all the data you provided me.

Lastly, I thank you, my dear reader, for picking up this book. I hope you enjoyed it as much as I loved writing it.

-Much Love,

Preethi Venugopala

SREEPURAM SERIES
Book 1: The Girl at the Wedding

A Sweet Romance Novella about Arranged Marriages, Family and Love.

Kishore is home on vacation after three years. To his horror, his family is determined to get him married this time. He creates the perfect plan to escape the matchmaking attempts of his family. Just when he thought he had everything under control, a girl from his past literally crashes into his life and turns his life upside down. Within a day, he is ready to sacrifice his bachelorhood entranced by the girl he meets at his friend's wedding.

One misstep and he acquire a rival. His own cousin, Abhishek.

What can he do to win back the love of his life?

Shreya can't believe that the handsome young man she is slowly falling in love with is the bully she hated in school. He has transformed in every possible way. She likes everything about him. But then something happens that prompts her to make a rash decision.

Would this one decision ruin her chances of finding true love?

Or would she have the courage to fight for love?

Book 2: Without You

Dr Arjun enters Ananya's life like a whirlwind, bringing with him the spirit of young love.

Does the path of true love ever run smooth? Circumstances force them apart even though they were irrevocably in love. She becomes a victim of depression. When everything fails to return her to normalcy, help

arrives from an unexpected source.
Will she ever find happiness again?

Will time allow her heart to heal and forget Arjun?

What indeed is true love?

What is that strange secret that locks all the circumstances together?

Travel with Ananya to the picturesque Sreepuram, face the chaos of Bengaluru, and relish the warmth of magical Dubai in this heart-warming tale of love, betrayal, friendship, and miracles.

Book 3: His Sunshine Girl

Can two damaged souls heal each other?

Shalini is dusky and has faced body shaming throughout her life because of it. She has gone through a lot in her life, including a failed marriage and divorce, and is at a crossroad when the story begins.

She arrives in Sreepuram as the live-in literary assistant to Arundhati Mukundan, an eminent author.

Dr.Vishal, Arundhati's grandson and a pediatrician, has seen love and loss at close quarters.

When they meet in Sreepuram, it is a reunion of two childhood friends who were once inseparable.

Will their friendship help them heal?

Isn't friendship turning into love the most beautiful thing on earth?

Would fate allow that to happen or would it play its devious role again?

This is a standalone sequel to the best seller 'Without You'. You can read this even if you haven't read 'Without You.'

This story picks up from where 'Without You' ended.

Look out for some of your favourite characters from 'Without You' taking on significant roles in this story.

Book 4: What the Stars Knew

Are our destinies written in the stars?

Meet two starcrossed lovers. Naveen and Arya.

One is a techie turned famed Vedic astrologer. The other is building her life back up from ashes.

Arya: Could someone shatter your heart into a million pieces with a single word?

Once, someone did that to me. I'd vowed to forget Naveen, became somebody else's forever only to realize that forevers don't exist.

I didn't realize the power of our shared memories until he returned.

And now, I can't stop myself from rushing into his arms.

I can't stop myself from falling for him all over again.

But Naveen is not the boy I once knew.

He now speaks of what the stars know, and unforeseen destinies.

All I care about is whether we have a future together.

Naveen: I won't survive if I lose Arya again.

The memory of us has hounded me for years.

I regret the moment I left her years ago.

I believed I could forget her.

But time has proven otherwise.

Her dark eyes still bewitch me, luring me into their depths.

But the stars tell me, she is not mine to cherish.

For the first time, I want to challenge them.

I want her to be mine forever.

What do the stars know?

What is written in the destiny of Naveen and Arya?

SRAVANAPURA ROYAL SERIES
Book 1: A Royal Affair

A British commoner in love with an Indian Prince

When Jane Worthington, a reporter with a London based entertainment channel, comes to India she is sure of two things.

Firstly, she would find Daniel Worthington, the lost twin of her beloved Grandfather and fulfill his last wish.

Secondly, now that she was in India, she was not going to think about Prince Vijay Dev Varman, the scion of the erstwhile royal family of Sravanapura, the man who broke her heart years ago.

Two seemingly impossible tasks.

Vijay always believed he knew everything about himself and his family. But when Jane storms back into his life, secrets tumble out one after the other disturbing the very thread of discipline that had granted his life a semblance of sanity.

Jane cannot refuse Vijay's offer of help but every moment with him is a torture because he is not the carefree youth she had once fallen in love with.

Will they succeed to find Daniel Worthington when every single trace of his existence seems to have been carefully wiped off by unseen hands?

Or will their quest reveal secrets that will make it impossible for them to even dream of a happily ever after?

A Suspense Novella about Second Chances in Love

Book 2: he Princess and the Superstar

A Princess in love with a Bollywood Superstar

Saketh Rao aka SR, India's latest Bollywood heartthrob, has bagged the role of a lifetime: to play Hari Varman, the doomed royal scion.

When he arrives at Sravanapura Palace with his director friend Rajeev Ratnam, little does he know that his life is about to change forever!

Princess Kritika is overjoyed that Saketh Rao will play the role of her ancestor. But when she comes face to face with the arrogant superstar she is determined to scuttle the project.

Fate, however, has different plans for them. The feisty couple is soon head over heels in love with each other.

As they uncover the secrets of Hari Varman's life, Saketh makes a discovery that can rip them apart and their new-found love.

Will the secrets and lies of the past deny them a future together?

Or will they overcome the obstacles to love?

Book 3: The Lost Princess

HOW FAR WOULD YOU GO TO PROTECT THE ONE YOU LOVE?

Ishaani, the newly crowned nightingale of the Indian music industry has it all: a dream career, a loving family and loyal friends. Yet, the man she has loved all her life will not warm up to her.

Rajeev, a hotshot movie director, has feelings for Ishaani. But, she is his sister's best friend and has been like another sibling to him. Yet, what can he do if he feels compelled to make her his own?

Then, Ishaani's life changes overnight. She is no longer a lowly commoner but a princess.

She has to make some tough decisions to protect the man she loves.

Her choices lead them both down a path filled with shocking revelations and devastating consequences.

Will true love prevail?

Or will the many twists of fate tear them apart?

Book 4: Love and Longing in Firefly Season

Rashi Ratnam, the newly minted design assistant of **billionaire fashion designer** Neel Mishra, is sceptical when she leaves on a field trip to Kerala with her temperamental boss.

It doesn't matter that she has been harbouring a crush on her gorgeous boss since forever.

The man intimidates her and is cold like ice.

Also, he hasn't still forgotten his ex-girlfriend.

At **Heaven's Cove**, the beautiful backwater island owned by Neel's grandparents, Rashi begins to see Neel in a new light. She also discovers his best-kept secrets.

It is the **firefly season**, and there is nothing that stops her from falling madly in love with Neel.

But **love** is not easy.

With Neel's jealous ex-girlfriend hovering around them stirring up troubles, life becomes strenuous.

Can they face the curve balls that fate throws at them?

Or will their love die a slow death?

But in the end, is the choice theirs to make?

Read this heartwarming contemporary love story of letting go and letting love in.

P.S: This book can also be read as a standalone romance. So, you can read this even if you haven't read the Sravanapura Royals series.

My Warmest Sorrow

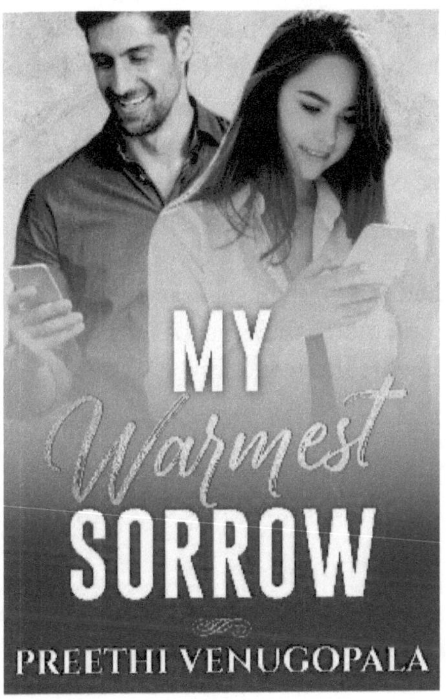

♥ **What would you do when you come face to face with your past?** ♥

Social media which is often a source of entertainment can be a source of great sorrow as well. Especially **alumni WhatsApp groups**, as not all memories are pleasant.

When Ajay, now an IAS officer, gets added to his **college** WhatsApp group, all his classmates welcome him warmly. Except for Jasmine.

Jasmine and Ajay were inseparable while in college. Their relationship had transitioned from being **best friends**

to lovers over the duration of the engineering course. But then **fate** had intervened, and they became estranged.

Five years of silence have created a **wall of sorrow** between them. Their interactions in the class WhatsApp group are nothing like what they once used to be. Every moment churns out more anguish and unpleasantness.

Jasmine is still living with the repercussions of what had happened in the **past**. Ajay's indifference throws her into despair.

What had caused their **separation**?

Is **love** still hiding underneath their public facades?

What **lies** are they concealing?

FALLING FOR CINDERELLA

When what you seek is seeking you...

Karan: It all started at a masquerade ball. I took one look at the girl dressed as **Cinderella** and fell **head over heels** in love.

I was not someone who believed in love.

Yet, within a few hours, she made me crave things I never knew I wanted.

I began to equate her presence with happiness.

Like a warm breeze on that winter night, she thawed my frozen heart.

At midnight, she ran away without telling me who she really was. Just like Cinderella.

I was never the same again.

I couldn't forget her, but she came visiting only in my dreams.

No matter what, I was determined to find her.

Chandni: Karan was not someone I could even dream about.

I was a poor orphan, a nobody.

He was a billionaire, the hottest bachelor in India, coveted by rich women everywhere.

A dance: that was all he asked.

But while we danced, I gave him my heart, knowing that the magic would end once he realized my true identity.

I was nothing but a cheat.

Yet, the **magic** didn't end that night.

A bizarre twist of fate put me in his path again. I had to hide my secret, even though I wished to confess everything to him.

Was watching him from afar the only thing that was written in my destiny?

Other Works By The Author

Short Stories
A Christmas in London
My Red Knight
Kid's Books
Anya and the Spring Fairy
The Teddy who ran away
Learn Malayalam Alphabets through Eng